VALINOR

Valinor

RICHARD J GUERIN

This book is dedicated to my mother Elizabeth and to all the mothers around the world. Like most mothers, she nurtured us from our early beginnings in life, provided us with love and comfort as we grew up, stood with us in adversity, shared in our accomplishments and showed us her love in many other ways. Although she has long since passed from this world, her love and the memories she gave us will always be there. Such is the priceless gift of having a mother and the priceless gift of their love.

Contents

Chapter 1: Skresh-Ka

Mars. By all outward appearances, an arid, desolate and lifeless planet, at least on the surface and from the perspective of those on Earth. Probes sent from Earth over the decades had only served to validate how inhospitable the planet could be. Far below the surface though, it is a different story. Teeming with life, it is home to an advanced civilization called the Skarzi. Ages ago, the Skarzi had come to this solar system and found the Annunaki, their ancient enemy, colonizing the habitable, third planet from the Sun. The fourth planet, while not ideal, was still a viable option. Settling below the surface, the Skarzi created a thriving colony there, far from their home world of Skarth in the Pleiades constellation. Following the same class system on their home world, the Skarzi on Mars had divided themselves into four clans. One was the

Sook warrior clan, another was the Sirk worker clan, and another was the Sath clan of scientists with the last being the Skom clan of political leaders.

Determined not to let the Annunaki control this star system, the Skarzi continued its age-old war here. With the Annunaki already colonizing the third planet called Earth, they became a constant threat to the Skarzi on Mars. In an effort to eliminate the threat, the Skarzi embarked on an ambitious plan to go on the offensive and destroy the Annunaki colonists on Earth. The Skarzi war machine went into high gear, producing huge warships and vast quantities of weapons. As the war machine ramped up production, it soon became apparent that there would be a shortage of personnel to operate the warships and use the waiting weapons. New breeding programs were initiated, with priority given to the Sook and Sirk clans in order to generate more warriors and workers.

A reptilian race, the Skarzi had evolved over millions years from dinosaurs into sentient beings. Walking upright, they appeared almost human-like from a distance. Close up however, they were much different. Oval shaped black eyes, finely scaled green skin and pointy reptilian teeth, these were just some of the differences from humans. Their ancestors the dinosaurs had become the leading life form on Skarth, unlike Earth where an asteroid had eliminated most of the dinosaurs, giving rise to mammals and eventually humans. Being reptilian in nature, the Skarzi birthed eggs instead of infants like humans. Evolution had reduced the ancient reptilian clutch of eggs to a single egg. Compensating for the single egg, evolution had in turn, allowed the Skarzi female to birth an egg every six months.

The order went out to every Sook and Sirk female of egg-laying age on Mars, to increase their egg production and contribute towards growing the population. Skarzi females, when the time came, gave birth to their egg at home and raised the young hatch-ling until the age of ten. Reaching that age, the young Skarzi were then sent to training facilities according to their clan. The groundwork having been laid, the Skarzi waited patiently, the war machine in full operation, building for that all important day of attack. That day eventually came and an armada of sixty Skarzi warships maneuvered towards Earth, confident in their success. Nearing Earth, the confident Skarzi reveled in the thoughts of destruction they would bring to the Annunaki.

Suddenly, a massive disturbance in the space facing the armada began to take place. Space began to waver and shimmer, the blackness of space turning a light blue, as massive warships began emerging from the wavering space. The Skarzi, taken by surprise, halted their advance towards Earth, trying to identify the emerging warships. Identification soon came in the form of energy weapons unleashed from the attacking warships. Many Skarzi warships were immediately destroyed, others fell away, hulls breached, spilling Skarzi into the airless void. The Annunaki fleet had arrived and the "Great Rout" had begun.

Eons in the future, Commander Skresh-Ka sat in a transport module, accompanied by two armed Sook warriors. The module zipped through the subterranean tunnels of Mars, heading to a meeting with leaders of the High Council. They refused to tell him what it was about, just that it was extremely important. Three thousand years ago, his distant ancestor, Captain Skresh had become both hero and legend, battling the Annunaki on the third planet in this solar system, called Earth. His ship, the Skyrim, had been destroyed along with everyone on board. In response, the Skarzi on Mars, had gone into an extended hibernation period, fearing a major attack by the Annunaki. No one had wanted to reprise the "Great Rout", which had occurred thousands of years earlier and had led to the decimation of almost the entire Skarzi population on Mars.

Skresh-Ka watched the tunnel lights whip past, as his transport module made its way along the vast, complex tunnel system connecting the different underground cities. That no one would say why he was being summoned, was concerning. It hinted at a need for secrecy. Skresk-Ka felt the transport module slowing as it reached the Skom city of Kraal. Gliding to a stop, the doors on the transport module slid open, revealing a line of Skom politicians patiently waiting for any available transport module. Skresh-Ka, followed by his warriors, stepped out of the transport module, sending whispers amongst the crowd. Skresh-Ka, dressed in full regalia, medals adorning his uniform, glinting in the artificial sunlight, had caught the attention of the crowd. That he was flanked by two armed, hulking warriors, only increased the whispers. Rarely was someone so prestigious from the Sook class seen here, causing the whispers to grow more excited. He blinked his reptilian eyes in the bright artificial sunlight, his warriors forcing a path through the crowd, as they hurriedly made their way to a waiting, automated ground car.

Climbing into the ground car, Skresh-Ka and his two warriors were whisked away to his meeting with the High Council. Upon arriving, Skresh-Ka and his warriors exited the ground car and stood in front of the imposing edifice. He had been here a couple of times, but the imposing nature of the building still caused some anxiety. A low level politician came out of the building, walking down the steps to greet the Commander.

"The High Council sends its greetings Commander. They are waiting inside for you. Please follow me", said the politician, his reptilian eyes blinking in the artificial sunlight.

Skresh-Ka and his warriors followed the politician into the building and into a grand meeting hall.

"The council is meeting in a smaller chamber. This way", motioned the politician.

They followed the politician to the smaller chamber and were greeted by two huge, closed, metal doors.

The politician pulled one of the huge doors open, clearly straining to do so.

"Wait here", hissed Commander Skresh-Ka to his warriors as he entered the smaller but still humbling chamber. Seated around him were the High Council members, supposedly from all the clans. Seated at the head of the council was High Lord Greesh-Ka, whose ancestor sub-lieutenant Greesh, had been killed aboard the Skyrim with Captain Skresh. Although their ancestors had shared a common bond, there was no such bond between the High Lord and the Commander. Each disliking the other for various reasons and yet respecting each other's places in society. The Commander always finding it odd that a member of the Sook clan had worked his way onto the High Council, a council comprised mostly of the Skom clan at the moment.

"Leave us and close the door", hissed High Lord Greesh-Ka to the politician, his reptilian eyes blinking in agitation.

Hurrying outside and closing the door behind him, the politician breathed a sigh of relief, happy to be outside.

"Welcome Commander. Thank you for agreeing to join us", hissed the High Lord.

"Why have I been summoned here?" asked Skresh-Ka.

"Always to the point, as usual. We have summoned you here because we have received a strange signal from the third planet. A signal that defies explanation and a signal that should not be", said the High Lord.

"Signal? What signal? Surely, you didn't summon me here just for some signal!" said Skresh-Ka, getting somewhat angry at a clear waste of his time.

"No need for belligerence. I assure you that this has implications for every Skarzi on this planet", hissed the High Lord.

"So what is this signal?" asked Skresh-Ka.

"Here's what we know: The signal is emanating from the third planet and from a desert area in the western United States. The signal appears to be coming from a Skarzi locator implant that was presumed destroyed three thousand years ago and in an area thousands of miles away from its current location. The unbelievable part is that the implant is from Captain Skresh. Yes, you heard that right, Captain Skresh, your ancestor", High Lord Greesh-Ka paused to let his words sink in.

Skresh-Ka stood there dumbfounded as he processed this unbelievable information. He wasn't surprised at the part about the western United States, since the Skarzi had been observing and adding to their extensive knowledge of Earth and the humans. He found it unbelievable that the implant signal was that of his ancestor, Captain Skresh, dead for some three thousand years. The implications weren't lost on Skresh-Ka. If it was Captain Skresh, it would rewrite Skarzi history on Mars, his family legacy and that of High Lord Greesh-Ka. Already called into question was how the Skyrim had actually been destroyed and how the crew had actually died. Did they really die a heroic death? Obviously, Captain Skresh couldn't be alive, could he? Skresh-Ka chose his next words carefully.

"What is it that you want me to do?" asked Skresh-Ka cautiously.

"I can tell from your lengthy delay in replying that you understand the implications of this. Legacies are at stake here, along with Skarzi history. The council has decided that we need to recover the implant and Captain Skresh, alive or dead. You will personally command a force to achieve this and deliver a plan to this council for final approval in 24 hours", said the High Lord.

"Very well, I will retrieve the implant and Captain Skresh, alive or dead", replied Skresh-Ka.

"Good. We are done here. You may leave", said the High Lord.

Skresh-Ka bowed and left the chamber, flanked by his two Sook warriors, lost in thought. He didn't know what dangers lay ahead, but was fairly certain it wouldn't be Annunaki, who were long dead by now. The humans though, had advanced technologically and could present some challenges. He really wasn't worried, since the Skarzi were orders of magnitude more advanced. There was a lot to do and not a lot of time, he thought, as he made his way back to the Sook capital and his command headquarters.

Chapter 2: Oversight

Martin sat in his underground office, leaning back in his chair, his fingers folded in front of him. He missed his daughter Pamela and felt an emptiness inside. Pamela and Trent were okay, but had taken leave from the DarkBridge facility for a European vacation. They would be gone for about a month, which hopefully, gave Trent some time to recover. Trent had been especially affected prior and during the TimeBridge mission. His body had been occupied by a demon named Lilith, who had caused a lot of trouble for the DarkBridge team. It was really Trent's own fault. In refusing to wear the protective ring, it had made him more susceptible to possession. Hopefully, Trent would realize his error and start wearing it when he returned. If not then Martin would be left with a difficult decision on whether to fire Trent or not. Martin wasn't sure how

Pamela would take the firing, but security was extremely important. He owed it to the people who worked here.

It was late afternoon, when Martin finally sent his report on what had transpired since receiving the signal from the Sinai Desert, to General Esterbrook and was waiting for a reply. He had left out a few things, mainly because they were fading memories, so much so that he doubted they had even happened. Like dreams that seem to fade away with the coming of morning. Things such as meeting his dead wife Susan and his sending the QASM bombs to different locations. He had also withheld Paul's discoveries in the Antarctic and had decided to transfer the entire contents of the cavern to the DarkBridge facility here. This would put the alien tech inside the continental United States and keep it out of foreign government hands. How they would still be able to keep it all secret, was another story. That was the plan, but as usual there was always a hitch.

"Martin. I've received word that General Esterbrook is arriving in your office shortly. He's bringing someone with him, but I don't have any further info on who it could be", said Eva, a touch of frustration edging into her voice.

"I've also received word that the transport team from Area 51 is here", said Eva.

"Thank you, Eva. Have Scott assist them in the transfer. I'll await the General's arrival", replied Martin, leaning back in his chair. When the alien body had been discovered inside the sanctuary, Martin had a hazmat team remove it, place it in cryogenic suspension and store it in the facility hospital. A twenty-four hour, seven days a week security watch had been set up just in case. Martin had included the alien discovery in his report, since it was more a job for Area 51. He'd heard reports of alien bodies being stored there and had asked General Esterbrook about it. The General had responded by saying it was "a need to know situation" and Martin really didn't need to know. Now, it looked like Martin knew without a doubt, of one alien body going there.

The four man transport team arrived via gateway in an unoccupied room in the hospital and waited for someone to take them to where the body was stored. They were wearing hazmat suits as a precaution against alien microbes.

"Hi. I'm Scott, your security liaison for this transfer", said Scott. Normally, he would've shaken their hands, but the suits precluded any such contact.

"Hello, Scott. We are the transfer team from Area 51", came the voice of the team leader through an external suit speaker.

"If you're ready, then follow me", said Scott, as he received a thumbs up from the four men.

Scott led them out of the room and down a hallway to a medical storage area where the body was stored and paused before the door. Placing his hand on the palm scanner first, he watched the palm pad turned green and then looked into the retinal scanner and stood still. The retinal scanner signaled a positive match. Passing both security checks, the door unlocked and Scott ushered the team inside and closed the door, waiting outside. The team of four took positions around the cryogenic chamber, disconnecting the pumps and electrical connections. The chamber, resting on a wheeled dolly, was now ready to move. A member of the team pressed a button on his suit radio and told Eva they were ready to leave. Eva, the coordinates already in memory, opened a gateway against a far wall, away from the team. The gateway shimmered a light blue color and quickly changed to a dark blue as it stabilized. Once stabilized, the team rolled the chamber through the gateway, presumably to a location somewhere inside Area 51. The transfer complete, Eva closed the gateway, notifying Scott who was waiting outside the room.

Martin received word from Eva that the transfer had been completed without incident. One less thing to worry about, thought Martin as he waited for the General to arrive. A flash of light from a far wall in his office caught Martin's eye and he watched as a gateway formed and stabilized. General Esterbrook stepped out, followed by a tall, slender woman, who looked to be in her early fifties, long dark hair cascading to her shoulders, a few streaks of gray showing. Martin silently gulped, finding the woman very striking.

"Hello, Martin. Good to see you. This is Dr. Natasha Zelensky, one of my top research scientists at Area 51", said General Esterbrook.

"Hello, Bob. Good to see you too. Welcome to DarkBridge Technology, Dr. Zelensky. I take it that this isn't a social call", replied Martin, finding it hard to keep his mind on the conversation. She certainly was striking, thought Martin.

"No, not social this time, but I am looking forward to another meal at Maggie's", replied the General with a smile.

"Anytime you like. I'm sure Maggie would be very pleased. So what brings you to DarkBridge?" asked Martin, his wariness growing. He liked Bob and they had become good friends over the years, but sometimes their jobs caused friction between them.

"I've read your latest mission report and so have my superiors. I'm feeling a lot of pressure from Majestic-12 to keep closer tabs on what goes on here. Oversight is the word, which brings me as to why Dr. Zelensky is here. She is going to be my liaison here, performing oversight on your facility. As far as you are concerned, it'll be business as usual, except that Dr. Zelensky will have some input and report back to me. I'm sorry about this Martin. In the eyes of Majestic-12, this is a rogue black site and needs oversight", said the General, letting it all sink in.

Martin was a little taken aback, but decided to hide his displeasure for now.

"Okay, Bob. I think we can accommodate Dr. Zelensky. I can appreciate the pressure you're under and will do everything I can to help", replied Martin. He needed to sound positive and cooperative. The US government was still his largest customer and he didn't want to jeopardize that relationship.

"Thank you, Martin. You're a good man and I assure you that this will work out. It's all about optics. I think I'm done here and need to get back to Area 51. The transport team has delivered the body to the examination room and I would like to be there. Take care, Martin. Natasha will remain here", said General Esterbrook, as the familiar shimmering gateway appeared.

"Take care, Bob. Let's schedule some time at Maggie's.", replied Martin, with a smile.

"I will Martin. Give Scott my regards. Take care Natasha, you're in good hands", said the General as he stepped through the gateway. The gateway winked out, leaving Martin and Dr. Zelensky alone.

Martin quickly broke the silence left by General Esterbrook with an olive branch.

"I'm looking forward to working with you Dr. Zelensky and will do everything possible to make your stay with us enjoyable, informative and you'll have our complete cooperation. I'm sure that Bob has told you something about me already, but I am in the dark about you", said Martin, hoping to get this oversight thing off to a good start.

"Thank you, Martin. Please call me Natasha. I'm Ukrainian by birth and hold US citizenship. I have doctorates in both theoretical physics and biomedical engineering. I have ultra, top secret security clearance and as you can see, the General trusts me", replied Natasha, her voice soft, but with a strong edge to it and a definite Ukrainian accent.

"Thank you, Natasha. I'm sorry for the third degree. As you can understand, I'm still processing all this and it might take a little time", said Martin. It was looking like his cavern plans were on hold for now.

"Maybe you could show me around your facility. You know, take a tour", suggested Natasha, observing that Martin was slightly older than she was, but was still rather handsome. The General had told her about Martin's wife dying in a car accident some years ago and how Martin subsequently threw himself into his work. Natasha would try to make this work, but wasn't entirely sure what her role was. Was she really just a spy?

"That's an excellent idea, Natasha. Let's take a walk", said Martin as he made his way around his desk. Walking towards the door, he opened it and stepped to the side. He ushered Natasha out, catching a whiff of perfume as she passed close by. They stood almost head-to-head and Martin found himself thinking about Susan and how lonely he had been without her. He closed the door behind them and led Natasha on a tour of the facility, thinking along the way of how complicated things had just become.

Chapter 3:
Natasha

Martin and Natasha walked down the hallway, reaching the small park, where he pointed out the various locations of interest.

"There's the theater, where we show recent movies and older movies including some movie marathons once in a while. Over there is the cafeteria, where all the meals and drinks are free, next to it is our recent addition, Maggie's, a great restaurant, where employees assume the cost of meals and drinks. Maggie Durham runs it and is a very special member of our team here", said Martin, pausing as he sensed that Natasha wanted to speak.

"Isn't she the daughter of Thomas Stanton, CEO of Stanton Aerospace?" asked Natasha.

"Yes. You are well informed. She prefers her married name of Durham. There's no love lost between her and Thomas Stanton. She's a true contributor here, both in restaurant operations and on our investigations team, with Paul Cross", replied Martin.

Natasha had heard about Maggie's, from people at Area 51 who had eaten there. All had given Maggie's high marks. Feeling ravenous, Natasha decided to check it out.

"Martin, I'm starving. Could we talk more over dinner?" suggested Natasha, her hopes high.

"Why certainly. I was going to suggest the same thing", replied Martin. This should be interesting, he thought to himself.

Martin led the way to Maggie's, holding the door open for Natasha and ushering her in.

Natasha found herself in what appeared to be a very nice restaurant, richly appointed, with tables in the center and booths arranged along the walls. Natasha was impressed. The hostess, seeing Martin walk in, immediately came over and took the two over to an unoccupied booth.

"Hello, Mr. Weaver. I'll let Maggie know you're here", said the hostess.

"Thank you, Sally. This is Natasha, who is going to be spending some time here at DarkBridge. I imagine that you'll be seeing much more of her once she samples the food", said Martin, smiling.

"Welcome, Natasha", said Sally, with a big smile.

"Thank you, Sally", said Natasha, also smiling.

Sally left to find Maggie, who came out of the kitchen, her blonde hair tied back in a ponytail. Waving at Martin, Maggie walked over to the table and took in the scene. Martin was seated across from an attractive, slender, dark-haired woman and her woman-sense detected something in how Martin was looking at the woman. Martin seemed to have a distinct sparkle in eyes.

"Hello, Maggie. This is Natasha. Natasha, this is Maggie, the owner and operator of this exquisite dining establishment. Natasha is joining us from Area 51, providing oversight on our various projects", said Martin quietly, as he introduced the two women.

"Thank you, Martin. Pleasure to meet you Natasha", said Maggie, with a smile. She wasn't sure what to make of the term "oversight" and its implications.

"Likewise", replied Natasha, thinking that she and Maggie could be good friends, once Maggie got over the distrust that Natasha sensed in the woman.

"I know what Martin is probably going to have for dinner, but what about you Natasha?" asked Maggie.

"Well, I've heard a lot about the prime rib here, so I'll try that. Medium rare and a glass of red wine", said Natasha, her mouth beginning to water. Her meals at Area 51 had consisted mainly of cafeteria food, so this promised to be a real experience.

"I'll have the usual, Maggie", said Martin, pleasantly surprised at Natasha's choice. He had thought her more of a fish or chicken person. Martin silently chided himself for being somewhat judgmental.

"I'll be right back with your drinks", said Maggie, as she turned and headed back towards the kitchen to place the orders. Moments later, Maggie returned, carrying a glass of red wine and a glass of beer for Martin.

"Thank you, Maggie", said both Natasha and Martin.

"You're welcome", replied Maggie, as she headed back to the kitchen.

"Welcome to DarkBridge Technology, Natasha", said Martin as he lifted his beer in a toast.

Natasha lifted her glass, causing a distinctive clink as it struck against Martin's.

"Thank you, Martin. This is quite the company you run here. I'm not entirely sure what the General expects of me, but I would like us to be friends", said Natasha with a smile.

"I'd like that as well, Natasha. It would be one less issue to worry about, considering the numerous other issues we face here. I'm not sure how much Bob has shared with you, but we'll try to fill in any gaps", said Martin, returning the smile, glad that Natasha had thrown out her own olive branch.

They chatted for a bit, with Martin finding out the Natasha's husband had died some ten years ago and Natasha hearing from Martin about the loss of his wife. Soon Maggie returned with two prime rib dinners, with Martin and Natasha both eyeing the plates with anticipation.

Natasha sliced into her prime rib with gusto, savoring that first bite, relishing its texture and flavor.

"This is absolutely delicious, Martin. Now I know why people love this place", said Natasha, as she took another bite.

"Yes, Maggie does a wonderful job running the restaurant and in making sure that every meal is delicious. Things like this make prolonged stays here more bearable", replied Martin, with a smile, as he noticed Natasha might finish her meal before him.

They chatted sporadically, between mouthfuls and soon both were finished with their meals. Maggie appeared shortly after, spotting the empty plates and smiling.

"Did everyone enjoy their meals?" asked Maggie, suspecting the answer would be a resounding "Yes".

"That was the most delicious prime rib I've had in a long time, Maggie. I think it's safe to say that you've gained another customer", said Natasha, her hunger satiated.

"It was another exquisite meal, Maggie. My compliments", said Martin.

"Thank you. It means a lot to me and my staff loves hearing it too. Can I get you anything else?" asked Maggie.

"I'm all set, Maggie", replied Natasha.

"That'll do it for me too. Just add this to my tab", said Martin, as he made a mental note to settle his growing tab.

"Sure thing. Let me get these dishes out of the way. It was nice meeting you, Natasha", said Maggie with a smile.

"Likewise", replied Natasha.

"Have a good night and thank you both for coming in", said Maggie, as she gathered up the dishes and carried them away. She had sensed that Martin wanted to leave, so she quickly returned to the kitchen.

They left the restaurant and Martin pointed out the other places of interest around the small park.

"There's a small pharmacy over there, where employees can purchase health items, medicines and small snacks. Next to it is the small hospital, run by Dr. Curtis", Martin paused, allowing Natasha to absorb what he had said.

"This is quite the place Martin. You really do a lot for the employees here", said Natasha, as she glanced around the park and the surrounding venues.

"Yes, we try. I have someone very important for you to meet. Eva?" said Martin, as he looked at Natasha. Alluring, was the word that came into his mind.

"Hello, Martin. Hello, Natasha", replied Eva, speaking through their implants.

"Hello, Eva. It's a pleasure to meet you. I've heard a lot about you from Adam", said Natasha, referring to the AI, Adam, at Area 51.

"Welcome to DarkBridge Technology, Natasha. If you need anything, just let me know", replied Eva.

"Thank you, Eva. I will", said Natasha.

"You'll find Eva to be extremely helpful. We consider her family around here", said Martin, with a smile.

"Why thank you, Martin", replied Eva.

"You're welcome, Eva. Have all Natasha's things been delivered to her apartment?" asked Martin.

"Yes, Martin. They were transferred from Area 51 a short time ago and I had them placed in Natasha's apartment", replied Eva.

"Excellent. Thank you, Eva", replied Martin.

"It's a lot to take in, Natasha. Why don't we continue the tour tomorrow, so that you can get settled in", offered Martin.

"Thank you, Martin. I must admit, I'm a little bushed, especially after such a delicious meal", replied a smiling Natasha.

"I agree, it has been a long day. Let me show you where you'll be staying", said Martin, returning the smile, as he led Natasha down a side corridor that connected them to the residential area. The side corridor soon opened up to the residential area, and after a few moments, they were at Natasha's apartment.

"Here we are Natasha. This is your apartment while you're with us. I think you'll find the accommodations satisfactory. If you need anything, you can ask me or let Eva know. I'll leave you to get some rest. I have to catch up on some business matters before retiring for the evening", said Martin.

"Good night, Martin. Thank you for the tour and dinner", said Natasha, with a smile.

"You're welcome, Natasha. Now get some rest and I'll see you in the morning", replied Martin, as he left Natasha and headed back to his office. She certainly was quite a woman thought Martin, noting a distinct spring in his step.

Natasha watched Martin leave, wondering at the responsibilities he must be shouldering. With a sigh, she entered her room, feeling a touch happier than she had in a long time.

Chapter 4: Memory Block

Vermont Guardian watched the events playing out in the DarkBridge facility above, the planet Earth and beneath the surface of Mars. Normally, it would've ignored Mars, but the Skarzi living underground appeared to be getting more active. Vermont, Negev and the other Guardians surmised that another attempt at war was coming from the Skarzi and without help, Earth would fall to them. Help would have to come from several sources, from the humans themselves, from the Annunaki Commander Kalon, who was still in suspended animation and possibly help from the angels. The demons were another matter and it would probably take a miracle to get them involved on the side of the humans. Vermont wasn't sure how much to expect from the angels, with their policy of not providing overt help, which mimicked the approach the

Guardians had towards humans. However, the angels Raphael and Gabriel seemed to be less strident about following that policy and often seemed to fall into a gray area, bordering on overt help.

Paul and Maggie would have their own roles to play, which is what Vermont was currently working on. Paul held memories of Valinor and he also held something else that perplexed Vermont. Ever since Valinor had come to Earth and had become known to Vermont Guardian, there was a memory that was blocked off to Vermont. No matter what Vermont did, access to this memory was blocked. Very frustrating to an advanced being like Vermont and showed a level of intelligence above that of the Guardians. Vermont had devised a plan to access that locked memory and at the same time, reawaken the Valinor memories of flying the Kyril spacecraft and his combat missions against the Skarzi. Vermont readied itself, as Paul and Maggie arrived at her apartment, both exhausted from the days events and were eager for some rest. The stage was set, as they retired to bed and fell fast asleep. Vermont waited patiently for Paul's mind to settle, before triggering the Valinor memories.

For Paul, It had been a long day, filled with mission reports and medical tests. Martin had allowed him some time to recover from the TimeBridge ordeal, but reality came knocking and people wanted answers. Everyone was still amazed that he had made it back safely from ancient Jerusalem and Dr. Curtis wanted to make sure that physically, he was okay. Paul was still at a loss as to how he came to be back at DarkBridge Technology, in perfect health and in the same timeline as he had been before stepping through the TimeBridge portal. He could see the frustration it caused in people, including Martin. All he could say, was that he had no memory of how he had been healed or how he had arrived, which was frustrating to him as well. Fortunately, the day was over and the bed welcomed him with promises of much needed sleep. It was an offer he couldn't refuse, as he laid down and sleep embraced him.

Darkness fell over Paul's mind and he fell into a deep slumber, his mind a blank canvas, waiting for dreams to be painted upon it. His breathing slowed and blurry images began to form as his dreams began. Maggie feel asleep almost immediately beside him, exhausted after a very busy day at the restaurant. Vermont waited expectantly for some idea of what was contained in that blocked off memory. Finally, after so many millennia, so many incarnations, Paul was about to give up that one secret memory withheld from Vermont. At least that was what Vermont was hoping for.

Chapter 5: Area 51

General Robert Esterbrook stepped out of the gateway and into his office located in the underground facility of Area 51. The office was utilitarian and sparsely furnished, with pictures of his family hanging on the walls. One of the pictures was of his son, Scott Esterbrook, taken as a group photo with the other members of his Navy Seal Team. Bob Esterbrook was proud of his son, as any father would be and that pride had never diminished. When Scott reached a crossroads in his career and left the Navy, Bob had suggested trying out a position at DarkBridge Technology. Martin needed an experienced person to fill a newly created position in security. Scott had accepted and as it turns out, was exactly the right fit for the job. Recent Dark-Bridge missions had only served to bolster that observation and Martin had expressed his thanks to

Bob on many occasions. Scott seemed happy with the position and for Bob, that was really all that mattered.

He settled into his leather chair, behind his desk and leaned back, glad to be off his feet. Martin had taken it well, considering the new oversight scrutiny he would have to deal with. Bob liked Martin a lot and considered him a good friend. Their friendship had grown over the years and each felt a high level of trust towards one another. Bob knew Martin had some secrets, which was okay, since Bob had quite a few off his own. However, his superiors at Majestic-12 would have none of that and considered DarkBridge Technology a rogue operation that needed to be reined in. In order to appease his superiors, Bob had offered Natasha as the face of that oversight and his superiors had willingly agreed. It had been their unanimous opinion that Dr. Zelensky would be the perfect choice, given her technical background and familiarity with the top secret operations at the different "black sites".

Bob let out a deep sigh, as his focus turned back to the matter of the alien body. There were other alien bodies stored here at the base, most recovered from crashed alien spacecraft. Martin had inquired about the alien bodies, but Bob had shut down any further attempts at learning more. Bob knew Martin would understand, each had their own jobs to perform. This alien body was different however, in that it wasn't recovered from a crash, but from one of the DarkBridge sanctuaries. Bob wasn't too clear on the sanctuary technology, except that it was a sort of safety refuge. The alien body also appeared to be three thousand years old, from what he had read in Martin's report on the TimeBridge mission. An examination of the body should prove most interesting, thought Bob.

"Adam. What is the status of the alien body retrieved from DarkBridge?" asked Bob. Adam was the AI at Area 51, performing similar functions as Eva did at DarkBridge.

"Welcome back, General. I trust your trip to DarkBridge went well. I'll miss having Natasha around. Our conversations were most enlightening at times. The alien body is being examined as we speak. Preliminary results show it to be wearing a self-healing type of organic body armor, comprised of talin, a self-healing material. It is impervious to most projectiles, except of course, a diamene coated bullet. The alien itself is reptilian, bipedal in nature and represents what could have arisen on Earth, if the dinosaurs had not died out and mammals had not taken over.

There was one surprise", said Adam, pausing to let the General absorb everything.

It took a few seconds for Bob to absorb everything, but Adam's last words caught his attention.

"What was the surprise?" asked Bob.

"We detected a signal being broadcast from a device embedded in the alien body. Evidently, the device draws power from any surrounding electrical field. Since it had been dormant for some three thousand years, it took some time for it to build up sufficient strength to broadcast", replied Adam.

"Broadcast? What is it transmitting?" asked Bob.

"Unknown. The signal is encrypted using an unknown format. We are working on a way to break the encryption, but without a language sample, we are at an impasse", replied Adam.

"What about the reception point? Do we know where it is being sent?" asked the General.

"The signal isn't powerful enough to reach any star systems other than our own. It would appear to be intended for someplace inside our solar system", replied Adam.

"I see. After three thousand years it's highly unlikely there's anyone around to receive it. However, please put the base on minimal alert status. Just in case", ordered the General.

"I agree. It's a prudent move. I'll let you get back to whatever you were doing", said Adam.

"Thank you, Adam. I'm just unwinding from my trip to DarkBridge. Keep me posted if there are any developments", said the General.

Bob settled back in his chair, thinking about what Adam had said. He'd read Martin's report on the TimeBridge incident and how an alien race called the Skarzi were involved. There had been a lot of information in that report and Bob wondered if the Skarzi had managed to populate a planet within this solar system. Surely, some sign of it would've been detected by now, given all the technological advances over the decades. This assumed they wouldn't mind being discovered, but what if they were purposefully staying hidden? Could they still be around after three thousand years? If they were, how would they react to the signal? Would they represent an existential threat to humanity?

Bob stifled a yawn and decided to grab a bite to eat from the base cafeteria. It was a pale comparison to Maggie's, possibly even no comparison, but it was nearby and he didn't want to return to DarkBridge just yet. Natasha and Martin needed to develop some sort of working relationship without him interfering. Bob thought about the pair, Martin having lost his wife and Natasha having lost her husband. Neither one was currently romantically involved and just maybe, Bob had subconsciously played potential matchmaker. Bob silently laughed to himself, wondering what Majestic-12 would think about that. Rising from his chair, Bob left his office, temporarily pushing these thoughts and others aside in order to enjoy a relaxing meal and hopefully a good night's sleep.

Chapter 6: Valinor

Paul, caught up in the dream triggered by Vermont Guardian, found himself dreaming of his past life as Valinor. He was in the pilot's chair of a spacecraft, similar to the five Kyril ships he'd seen in the Antarctica cavern. His Kyril spacecraft appeared to be speeding towards combat against a large Skarzi space fleet. A glance out the cockpit window showed dozens of other Kyril spacecraft following his lead, the vastness of space surrounding his spacecraft. He appeared to be the "tip of the spear", leading the other combat spacecraft into battle. The Skarzi fleet looked impressive on his advanced Annunaki sensors, but equally impressive was the Annunaki battle fleet following behind him. Valinor smiled at the shock that was waiting for the Skarzi, when they learned that Commander Kalon was personally in command of the Annunaki fleet.

A military legend among the Annunaki, Commander Kalon had been responsible for many of the defeats suffered by the Skarzi.

The Skarzi fleet soon came into view, sixty large battle cruisers arrayed themselves before the Annunaki fleet, spewing out swarms of smaller attack fighters. Valinor gave the order to engage and the other pilots followed Valinor, meeting the Skarzi fighters in a blaze of weapons fire. The combat appeared to be one-sided, with the energy weapons of the Skarzi fighters falling away harmlessly, against the advanced shielding of the Annunaki Kyril fighters. Valinor and his squadron of Kyril fighters, firing the advanced Annunaki weapons, sliced through the Skarzi fighters like a hot knife through butter. The Skarzi fighters fell away in droves, while the Annunaki battle cruisers began firing their massive particle beam weapons at the Skarzi fleet. In a move straight out of the Commander Kalon playbook, two other Annunaki battle fleets appeared, flanking the Skarzi fleet on either side and firing their own particle beam weapons.

One by one, the Skarzi battle cruisers began falling away, explosions rocking cruisers hit by the Annunaki weapons. Outmatched and outgunned, the enemy battle cruisers began falling away, heavily damaged and inoperable, some exploding altogether, casting metal debris and occupants into the dark, airless void of space. For the Skarzi it was an unmitigated defeat, falling into a trap laid by perhaps the greatest military commander of all time. Valinor would've given anything to be on the bridge of a Skarzi battle cruiser when the Annunaki fleets suddenly appeared. Commander Kalon must be relishing in the inevitable Skarzi defeat, he thought to himself. Suddenly, two Skarzi combat fighters came at him, firing their weapons, confident that the Annunaki facing them would be destroyed. Unfortunately for them, the advanced Kyril battle armor held up to their withering fire and Valinor unleashed his own form of destruction. The two Skarzi fighters exploded into clouds of debris, with their pilots vaporized in an instant.

Valinor kept one eye on the larger battle, while continuing to destroy the Skarzi fighters arrayed in front of him. A Skarzi pilot, seeing the futility of using inferior weapons against the Annunaki, decided on a brute force approach. Signaling four other fighters to join him, they plunged on a suicide mission, towards the lead Annunaki fighter. Valinor, being the lead fighter, was engaged in destroying the remaining Skarzi fighters and didn't see the approaching suicide fighters in time. Two of his Annunaki wing men, saw the five Skarzi fighters approaching at high speed and managed to destroy two of the fighters, but three made it through, impacting Valinor's Kyril spacecraft at high velocity. The ensuing brilliant flash of the explosion temporarily blinded the wing men. When the explosion and debris finally cleared, there was no sign of Valinor or his fighter. Presumed dead and the spacecraft utterly destroyed, the two wing men notified the Annunaki fleet of Valinor's loss. The Skarzi, sensing defeat on the battlefield, recalled their fighter craft and began pulling away at high speed, fleeing to the safety of a nearby solar system. Remnants of destroyed Skarzi battle cruisers littered the battlefield, continuing to burn and explode, as fires reached ammunition and fuel storage areas.

Here it was. Finally, here was the memory that Vermont Guardian had tried for so long to see. It delved into that memory, but just as in the attempts before, it was repulsed. This time though, a more forceful energy pulse enveloped Vermont Guardian, temporarily paralyzing it. Paralyzed and bewildered, Vermont thought it had made a mistake with devastating consequences, as a simultaneous effect was felt by the other Guardians on Earth and on the Moon. Vermont feared that somehow their prisoner, Lucifer, would take advantage of the paralysis and escape, thus dooming the universe.

The effect wasn't lost on Lucifer, who felt a lessening of the Guardians hold on him. "What had caused this?" thought Lucifer to himself. He tested the shackles of energy holding him and as they glowed a brilliant red, he sensed a weakness in those bindings, a weakness that could be exploited. The shackles were still too strong to break, but this event left him hopeful that there was a means to escape. If only he could find out what it was that caused it, then he could replicate the effect, but this time with more power. He felt the effect soon wear off though, as the five Guardians returned to fully powering his shackles. "Most interesting", said Lucifer to himself.

Vermont Guardian felt the temporary paralysis fade away, leaving it with no ill effects. Vermont immediately recoiled from the dream, which Paul was still engaged in. What had caused the paralysis? How had it been done? The "why" was pretty obvious. Someone or something didn't want the contents of the dream known and had both knowledge and power beyond that of the Guardians. The other Guardians were expressing their own concern and signaled the need to halt any further studies of the dream until they understood what had happened. Vermont complied, considering the precarious position the paralysis had left the Guardians in. What if next time, the effect was even more powerful and damaging? No, there was too much at stake, so Vermont allowed Paul to continue with the dream without further interference.

Chapter 7: Survivor

Valinor couldn't believe he was still alive, or at least thought he was still alive. How could he have survived the impact of three Skarzi spacecraft? He was no longer sitting inside his fighter, but standing outside of it surrounded by a white void. It was all white, as far as he could see and the atmosphere breathable, since he wasn't wearing a helmet. Only he and his black, Kyril spacecraft marred the pristine whiteness surrounding him. He must be dead and this is what heaven must be like, was his first thought.

"No. You're not dead", came a soft, but commanding reply.

"Where am I and what do you want?" asked Valinor, who found it unsettling to have his thoughts read.

"You are nowhere. This place exists so that we may communicate. I have brought you here because you have a destiny beyond that of your current lifetime. In doing so, your life was saved from being utterly destroyed", said the same voice.

"I thank you, but who are you? asked Valinor, who was trying to absorb what was happening.

"For purposes of this conversation, you may call me Celestra", said the voice, except this time a tall woman with long, flowing dark hair came striding out of the whiteness. She was wearing a long white gown that seemed to sparkle, almost like it was made of tiny stars. Wearing golden sandals, she approached Valinor, halting a few feet away.

"Hello, Valinor", said Celestra, in the same soft and commanding voice.

Valinor, captivated by her beauty, could barely manage to speak, "Hello, Celestra".

"I'll try and answer some of your questions, but some questions must remain unanswered for now. I am what could be called a celestial being, my father being the Creator himself. As I said earlier, I have intervened to save your life in order to preserve your destiny, which fits in with my plans. Normally, I wouldn't have intervened, but you and someone you will someday meet, form a nexus, where events will revolve around the two of you. That's as much as I can say for now, except that interesting times are in store for you both in this life and beyond", said Celestra, allowing some time for Valinor to process what she had said.

"When can I return to my squadron?" asked Valinor. He was beginning to find Celestra's beauty very beguiling.

"There are a couple of things to take care of before you leave. First, your spacecraft is too pristine and would certainly arouse suspicion", said Celestra, as she began inflicting damage to the Kyril spacecraft.

Valinor watched in disbelief, as parts of the spacecraft crumpled and dented, as if some mighty hand had begun crushing it. He saw a wing begin tearing off, the advanced diamene armor being no match for the power Celestra was wielding.

"Your ship now looks like it had indeed been struck by the enemy spacecraft I saved you from. It is time for you to get back to your life. You won't remember this conversation, but your future reincarnations will, once the memory is accessed. The interior of your ship is still structurally intact, airtight and will keep you alive until you are found. Have a good life, Valinor", said Celestra with a smile.

Valinor smiled back, just as a wave of blackness fell over his mind and he felt himself go unconscious.

Celestra waved her hand causing Valinor to disappear and reappear back inside his spacecraft. Finally, with a last wave of her hand, the spacecraft with Valinor safely inside, disappeared, leaving Celestra surrounded by unmarred, pristine whiteness.

Valinor fought his way back to consciousness, gradually becoming aware of his surroundings. He blinked a few times, his eyes focusing on the view outside the cockpit. His spacecraft appeared to be floating near the mangled wreck of a Skarzi battle cruiser. Large pieces of debris drifted about and Valinor hoped none of it struck his spacecraft. With a missing wing and other control surface damage, there wasn't much he could do to maneuver around the debris. He couldn't remember anything after what should've been certain death from the impact of three Skarzi fighters. How had he survived? He started to ponder the question, but suddenly, a voice called out from his communications console.

"Captain Valinor. Can you hear us? Are you okay?" said the voice.

"Yes. I'm still alive and surprisingly unhurt, but my ship has been heavily damaged and I'm unable to maneuver", replied Valinor.

"Glad to hear you're still alive Captain. This is Captain Jalon of the light cruiser Mystral. We'll be rescuing you shortly. Good thing we were in the area on patrol", said Captain Jalon.

"Thank you, Captain. I was starting to get nervous out here", replied Valinor, who thought he heard cheering in the background. Valinor was impressed. None other than Commander Kalon's son was coming to rescue him. His sensors soon detected the approach of the light cruiser, which released two space tugs with grappling arms to retrieve his spacecraft. Valinor felt a sense of relief when the tug's grappling arms locked onto his ship and began towing him towards the hangar bay of the cruiser. Once inside, the tugs slowly lowered Valinor's ship to hangar floor, with the hangar doors closing behind them. Valinor let out a deep breath, happy to be alive.

Paul stirred from the memory, but not before a final thought came to him,

"Hello, Paul. My name is Celestra and I'll be seeing you very soon".

Paul's eyes sprang open and he quickly sat up in bed, his eyes scanning the room for any intruders. The voice had been crystal clear, as if it were coming from this very room. He turned and looked at Maggie, who was still sleeping soundly. He was glad that she hadn't awakened, since her day had been very busy and she needed some rest. Wary, he slowly laid back down in bed, processing the dream he just had. There had been a lot of information contained in the dream and he was glad that he possessed a photographic memory. With some help from Raphael or Gabriel, he just might be able to fly one of the Kyril fighters stored in the Antarctica cavern if it became necessary. It was still a few hours before he needed to get up, so he tried falling back to sleep. Fitfully at first, sleep gradually overcame him.

Vermont Guardian sensed that Paul had abruptly woken from the dream. Obviously something had startled him awake, something in the dream. Vermont was hesitant to access Paul's memory of that particular dream, fearing that another attempt might harm it and the other Guardians even more severely. Vermont had found itself apologizing profusely to the other eleven Guardians for any harm it may have caused. Paul appeared to have been jolted out of bed by the memory, but had since settled down, falling back to sleep. Vermont puzzled over what had happened, promising to itself and the other Guardians to be more cautious with Paul's dreams in the future. With nothing more to be done at this time, Vermont settled back into watching the events occurring above.

Chapter 8: Preparations

Commander Skresh-Ka looked at the attack plans displayed above his desk, his reptilian eyes blinking every so often. While it was theoretically a recovery mission, there was no doubt that some resistance would be met. The place on Earth known as Area 51 would be defended, but the extent of that defense was open to speculation. That and other areas on Earth had been under surveillance for many human decades by the Skarzi and much had been learned. The humans at Area 51 seemed to be holding various elements of alien technology and there seemed to be other locations on Earth that were of interest as well. Whether the humans had discovered how that technology worked or had developed weapons from it, remained to be seen. It wasn't an ideal situation, with so many unknowns, but Skresh-Ka had complete confidence in the Skarzi technological dominance over the primitive technology of the humans.

The plan was simple, go in, locate Captain Skresh's transmitter and recover the remains or however improbable, Captain Skresh himself. Skresh-Ka found the latter highly unlikely, hissing to himself with its absurdity. Most likely, only the transmitter had been found and was being examined by the humans. Six ships would be needed, one battle cruiser, three scout ships and two assault troop transports. Four hundred assault troops would disembark, secure the area and a smaller force would make its way into the underground facility, following the transmitter signal of Captain Skresh. The ships would be cloaked to evade the primitive human radar systems and help guarantee a surprise attack on the humans. Additionally, meta-material cloaking technology would render all surface ships and assault troops invisible to the human eye, adding to the surprise. The humans would never know what hit them, thought Skresh-Ka to himself.

Operational security would be provided by the battle cruiser and scout ships would provide security and protection for the assault troops. The signal was probably coming from underground, so the assault force would break into the tunnel system and breach the facility. It was a good plan, but Commander Skresh-Ka would've preferred a more covert approach with a smaller force, but with so many unknowns and the need for a successful recovery, this brute force approach was required. Satisfied, Commander Skresh-Ka sent the plan to High Lord Greesh-Ka and the Council for approval. Much was riding on the success of this mission and High Lord Greesh-Ka had made it plain that Skresh-Ka should take personal charge of the mission. That the Skarzi here hadn't seen any actual combat in thousands of years worried Skresh-Ka. His forces had trained, but nothing beat actual combat experience. Skresh-Ka hoped the losses would be acceptable.

Minutes later, a message came back from High Lord Greesh-Ka, "Proceed without delay and take personal charge. Good luck, Commander". Skresh-Ka looked at the message and let out a hiss. High Lord Greesh-Ka hadn't wasted any time in responding. Yes, a lot was riding on this mission, mostly his reputation and he needed to come through this with a victory. Anything less would be very, very bad for him. High Lord Greesh-Ka would be waiting to deliver his sentence upon return. Skresh-Ka hissed to himself and stood up from his desk, medals clinking across his uniform and signaled for his personal guard. It was time to go.

Raphael and Gabriel stood on the surface of Mars, unfazed by the lack of oxygen and oblivious to the cosmic rays bombarding them. A small dust devil formed nearby, stirring the Martian soil and sending reddish particles of soil into the air. They gazed out over a wide Martian plain, broken only by a deep, wide canyon.

"Do you sense it?" asked Raphael.

"Yes, I sense some sort of activity going on below the surface", replied Gabriel.

"The activity seems to be centered around or near the Sook area", said Raphael.

"The warrior class?" asked Gabriel. Both angels were familiar with the four classes of Skarzi hierarchy, due to their former lives as Annunaki.

"Yes, that's it exactly. We may have a problem. Let's take a closer look", replied Raphael.

The two angels drifted down into the canyon, quickly reaching the rock strewn bottom, tall vertical walls soared up from the bottom on either side.

Raphael's words proved prophetic, as a huge portion of the canyon wall facing them, split open vertically and each side slid apart, revealing a massive underground hangar. As the two angels watched, six spacecraft drifted out of the immense hangar and into the wide canyon. Having discharged the spacecraft, the canyon wall slid closed, appearing once again, as a normal, nondescript rocky wall. The six spacecraft silently rose into the air, with Gabriel and Raphael watching from the canyon floor. Increasing their speed, the six spacecraft soon reached the upper reaches of the thin Martian atmosphere. The two angels rose into the air, following the departing spacecraft into low Martian orbit and watched as five of the spacecraft turned towards Earth. The remaining, sixth spacecraft headed in the opposite direction towards the asteroid belt between Mars and Jupiter.

"Where do you think they're going?" asked a curious Gabriel.

"Most likely Earth", said Raphael, as he and Gabriel drifted higher, leaving the planet Mars slowly rotating beneath them.

"What about that single spacecraft heading towards the Asteroid Belt?" asked a curious Gabriel.

"That one is interesting. I'm sensing multiple energy sources hidden within the Asteroid Belt. That is where the Skarzi hid their battle fleet in the Great Rout, so many thousands of years ago", replied Raphael.

"It seems a little suspicious. There must be something out there. Otherwise, why would the shuttle head out there?" asked a curious Gabriel.

"We should follow it", suggested Raphael.

"I agree", replied Gabriel.

The two angels followed the lone Skarzi space-craft into the Asteroid Belt, watching the shuttle carefully thread its way through asteroids of various sizes, avoiding any change to their trajectories. Soon their suspicions were verified as the two angels spotted a hulking battle cruiser hidden among the asteroids. The Skarzi spacecraft was headed directly towards it and the two angels sensed multiple battle cruisers hidden among the Belt.

"It appears our suspicions are correct. There is a sizable battle fleet hidden here and it's a definite danger to Earth. The humans would have little chance of survival", said a somber Raphael.

"Well, we know where this spacecraft went, but what about the other five?" asked Gabriel.

"Yes. We should verify that Earth is their destination", replied Raphael, as he opened a gateway and the two angels stepped through.

The gateway opened high above the planet Mars and the two angels stepped out into the black void of space, with the planet Mars slowly rotating below them. The five Skarzi spacecraft were now a few thousand miles beyond the orbit of Mars and appeared to have paused, as if waiting for something or someone.

"From the heading they appear to be taking, I would say Earth is their destination", said Raphael.

"I agree. There seems to be something else. There's a thin silver line connecting the Earth to Mars", replied Gabriel, his senses tuned to things beyond what humans could see.

"Yes, I see it. A communications signal of some sort and the Skarzi spacecraft appear to be following it", said Raphael.

"We should look for the origin point on Earth", suggested Gabriel.

"Excellent idea. It's obviously trouble for someone on Earth, but maybe there's something we can do about it", replied Raphael, as he opened another gateway, this time exiting above the Earth.

"The Skarzi have increased speed and will reach Earth in a few hours. I'm sensing a larger ship has joined the five and all the ships are now cloaked to avoid detection. Do you see the point of origin?" asked Raphael.

"Yes. The American southwest, in a place the humans call Nevada. The origin point is a secret government facility called Area 51. I believe Paul worked there before joining DarkBridge Technology", replied Gabriel.

"Most interesting. Hopefully, the Skarzi don't extend their operation to DarkBridge", said Raphael.

"I wonder what the Skarzi want there? It's already getting dark at Area 51 and with the Skarzi ships cloaked and arriving soon, the humans won't see them in time to defend themselves", replied Gabriel.

"Yes, the humans will be caught off guard and some will probably die. With regards to the signal, it's Skarzi and the only Skarzi on Earth that I know of is the one that was in Paul's sanctuary. It must have been moved", replied Raphael.

"It must be the body of Captain Skresh according to what Paul recounted. The Skarzi were known for having homing beacons implanted in their bodies for tracking. In case of injury or death they could be retrieved", replied Gabriel.

"Three thousand years ago I sent a message before destroying the Skarzi ship, Skyrim. That seemed to keep them away until now. Maybe it's time to send another message. Since we can't directly interfere, we'll need to enlist the help of someone", said Raphael.

"Sounds like you have a plan", said Gabriel.

"Yes and it involves Paul", replied Raphael.

"Paul? What can Paul possibly do against the Skarzi", asked a puzzled Gabriel.

"You forget the five Kyril spacecraft in the Antarctica cavern. Paul has Valinor's memories, which makes him the best choice. He can fly one Kyril fighter and the other four can be slaved to his ship, effectively giving him control of five combat ships", said Raphael.

"Yes, that could work. I would love to see the look on the Skarzi commander's face when five Annunaki spacecraft appear out of nowhere", replied Gabriel.

"We must hurry. The Skarzi will be here soon and there is much to do. One of us will have to go to Antarctica and get the spacecraft flight ready and the other will have to get Paul ready", said Raphael.

"I'll take care of Paul. We'll also need to get the gateway generator operational in the Antarctica cavern. ", replied Gabriel.

"Yes, we need that gateway to get those ships out of the cavern. I'll take care of the cavern. Make sure Paul is ready to fly", said Raphael.

"Sounds like a plan to me. See you soon, my friend", replied Gabriel, as he opened a gateway to the DarkBridge facility.

Raphael watched his fellow angel leave, unsure as to how Vermont Guardian would react to their plan. There wasn't time to consult with Vermont and they were already running out of time. Hopefully, Paul would agree and remember how to fly the Kyril fighter. So many unknowns", thought Raphael to himself, as he opened a gateway to the Antarctica cavern and stepped through.

Vermont Guardian watched, as the two angels began putting their plan into action. The plan wasn't without some danger to Paul, but Vermont had taken a more "hands off" approach to events involving Paul. It was in response to their last meeting, where Vermont had saved Paul from dying in his sanctuary. 'Free will" had been discussed and the right for Paul and Maggie to choose where they stayed during the intervening times between reincarnations. It was difficult for Vermont to remain detached, after having bonded with the two former Annunaki so many millennia ago. As far as Paul's knowledge of piloting the Kyril spacecraft, Vermont sensed some knowledge left behind in Paul's mind from his recent dream. Vermont hadn't put it there, but it was there. A disconcerting thought occurred to Vermont, "what if someone or something else was involved in helping Paul"? Vermont's thoughts grew troubled, as he watched events unfold.

Chapter 9:
Assault Force

Commander Skresh-Ka sat facing the forward view screens, watching as the pilot deftly dodged a looming asteroid that had crossed paths with the shuttle. In the distance, Skresh-Ka could just make out the hulking battle cruiser Ketska. It was one of forty battle cruisers hidden amongst the asteroid belt, just waiting to be deployed. Some were still under various stages of construction and others completed. Skresh-Ka was proud of his fleet and of the Sook warriors who currently manned the ships. The fleet had grown since the time of the Great Rout, with each successive generation inheriting the gains of the prior one and a ship or two added with each generation. Great care had been exercised in rebuilding the fleet, so as not to attract the attention of the Annunki, even though it had been quite some time since they were last seen.

Having all these ships was one thing, manning them to a hundred percent was another, with some of the ships only staffed at twenty-five percent, due to warrior shortages. More Sook warriors would have to be hatched, mused Skresh-Ka.

The shuttle rapidly closed the distance and was soon dwarfed by the massive battle cruiser as it maneuvered into the large docking bay. Once safely inside, the docking bay doors closed and the bay repressurized, allowing Commander Skresh-Ka to exit the scout ship. He made his way to the bridge of the battle cruiser, crew members lining the corridors, saluting as he passed by. Reaching the spacious bridge, Skresh-Ka paused at the wide doorway, surveying the bridge crew at work while waiting for the ship's Captain to greet him.

"Welcome, Commander. It is a pleasure and an honor to have you aboard", said Captain Breesh, as he saluted the Commander.

"Thank you, Captain. I trust all is ready and we can depart?" said Skresh-Ka, as he entered the bridge.

"Yes Commander. We're ready", replied Captain Breesh, his reptilian eyes blinking.

"Very good. Engage stealth mode and rendezvous with the assault force, which is also in stealth mode and will be waiting for us. The humans will never see us coming", said Skresh-Ka, a look of satisfaction showing on his reptilian face.

"Yes Commander", replied Captain Breesh, who began issuing commands to the bridge crew. Warning alarms sounded throughout the ship, as the Ketska' s massive engines powered up and the ship began threading its way through the asteroid belt, maneuvering between the rocky field before it. Soon, the huge warship was out of the asteroid belt and on its way towards a rendezvous with the assault force.

Skresh-Ka watched the view screens as the asteroid belt rapidly fell behind the accelerating Ketska. Mars, just a small reddish orb on the view screens, began to grow larger, filling the screens, growing smaller as the Ketska passed by.

"Commander, we are approaching the assault force", said Captain Breesh.

"Excellent news, Captain. We will rendezvous and the entire assault force will journey towards the planet Earth and our target", replied Skresh-Ka.

"Yes, Commander", said Captain Breesh, as he issued additional commands to the bridge crew.

It didn't take long, before the assault force showed up on the Ketska view screens. Modified to view ships that were cloaked and in stealth mode, the screens showed tiny points of light, growing larger and larger, until the Ketska reached the assault force.

"Captain, I wish to deliver a message to the ships. Can you patch me through?" asked Skresh-Ka.

"Yes Commander. Ready", replied Captain Breesh, as he gave orders to the comms officer.

"Thank you, Captain. Attention all ships. This is Commander Skresh-Ka. Our target is a military installation on Earth that we believe is secretly developing technology to attack our Skarzi cities on Mars. Your squad leaders and ship captains have been briefed on the assault plans and will brief you before the assault. Every one of you will be contributing to the greater glory of the Skarzi. We will teach these humans a lesson they will never forget! Long live the Skarzi!" Skresh-Ka ended his speech with a wave to Captain Breesh, who ended the call.

"Captain Breesh, adjust our speed so that we arrive on target at midnight local Earth time. Have the assault force fall in behind us. The Ketska will lead them into battle", said Skresh-Ka.

"Yes, Commander", replied Captain Breesh, his dark eyes blinking with excitement at the upcoming carnage.

Skresh-Ka sat back in his chair mulling over his speech. He had lied somewhat in saying that the humans were preparing to attack Mars. He still needed to hide the true reason for the attack and once on the ground, only a highly trusted team of Sook warriors would look for the transmitter and either Captain Skresh or his remains. To Skresh-Ka, there were still too many unknowns and he hoped that no surprises awaited them. The last thing he wanted was to lose face in front of High Lord Greesh-Ka.

"Captain Breesh. I'll be in my quarters. Alert me when we arrive", said Skresh-Ka, as he rose from his chair.

"Yes, Commander", replied Captain Breesh.

Skresh-Ka left the bridge, crew members saluting him as he passed by. He returned the salutes, but was eager to get to his quarters and get some rest before the anticipated assault. Since making the Ketska his flagship during its design, Skresh-Ka had made sure his quarters were well appointed. Reaching his quarters, he paused briefly at the door, as the ship AI verified it was him. The door slid open and closed behind him, as he immediately made his way to the large, luxurious bed. Lying down, his thoughts drifted to those of his partner, Sareesh back on Mars. They had been together for many solar cycles and Sareesh had given birth to ten hatchlings so far, with another on the way. Sareesh was a good mate and he missed her greatly. She never complained about his extended absences, due to his high position and always greeted him warmly when he returned. Skresh-Ka was extemely pleased that he would have heirs to his family's legacy and the status it would give them in Sook society. Content, Skresh-Ka slowly dozed off, thoughts of a glorious victory filling his mind.

Lucifer watched the events unfolding on Mars from his prison deep within the Moon. Long ago, he had set the Skarzi on the road to war with the Annunaki, in order to see who was the stronger. It was his right after all, since he was a superior being. He'd been greatly pleased when the Skarzi had arrived on Mars, so many eons ago, and set about building a civilization to rival the Annunaki on Earth. The Skarzi were the foil to the Anunnaki on Earth and a recurring pain in their proverbial backsides. The humans, with their lack of understanding the issues with time travel, had inadvertently set in motion a series of events that would ultimately lead to war with the Skarzi. The removal of Captain Skresh's body from their primitive dimensional sanctuary had allowed the implanted tracking device to activate and start broadcasting.

Personally though, any conflict between the humans and Skarzi would be still be meaningless to his current situation as a prisoner. The conflict wouldn't release him, but would be a great distraction to the Guardians, who might become distracted enough to allow him to escape. Compounding his problem of escape, was the fact that the Skarzi had yet to have any working knowledge of making dimensional gateways. Had they developed this technology, then he could entertain the thought of rescue, even Asmodeus and his demons were of little help. The five Guardians holding him prisoner could easily thwart any attack on his prison by Asmodeus and his demon minions.

There was one being that could possibly help free him and that was Black. Lucifer had sensed Black leave Earth for Mars some three thousand years ago. After a brief period of time, Black had left Mars and the solar system, heading towards the Pleiades constellation. Lucifer assumed it had something to do with the Skarzi, since their home world was located there along with the Annunaki home world. In the intervening time, Lucifer had forgotten about Black. Now, although limited by captivity in what he could do, Lucifer pushed against those boundaries and cast his mind out towards the Pleiades constellation.

There he found Black, who appeared to be headed back to Earth for some reason. Finding Black wasn't what had really surprised him, for in casting his mind out, he had sensed a power equal to his own or greater. Lucifer quickly pulled his mind back in order to remain hidden, but it was too late, the entity had detected him and was coming. For the first time since his creation, he felt fear and a sense of helplessness. As a prisoner, there was nothing he could really do, except wait. Maybe his Guardian captors would help protect him, then again maybe not. Conserving his energy, Lucifer could only wait and hope that the entity was friendly.

Chapter 10: Drafted

Paul just couldn't get back to sleep. The dream about Valinor had totally unnerved him. It was Celestra that really bothered him. It had been a dream about Valinor and yet she had said "Paul". More worrying, it was as if she knew who he was and where he was. Paul had no doubt that Celestra was indeed coming. The question was whether she would be friend or foe. Even with the technology at hand and some angel help, Paul wasn't sure there would be anything they could do to stop her, if it came to that.

He glanced over at the alarm display and saw that it was about 11:50 pm. Turning, he saw that Maggie was thankfully still sound asleep. That was good. No need for her to get worried about something that could just turn out to be a bad dream. As he lay there in bed, Paul began to notice the faint golden glow of a gateway beginning to form in a corner of the bedroom. A split second later, the gateway turned a bright, golden yellow and a figure stepped out.

"Gabriel?" whispered Paul.

"Hello, Paul", replied Gabriel, as he stepped over to Maggie and gently waved his hand over her forehead.

"She is in a deep sleep now and won't be awakened by us, as we talk. It's good to see you Paul, but I wish it were under more pleasant circumstances", said Gabriel, as he straightened up to look at Paul, who had climbed out of bed.

"Time is critical, so I'll get right to the point. Very shortly, the Skarzi will be staging an assault on Area 51. It appears that they want to retrieve the Skarzi body that was found in your sanctuary. People are going to die, that much is certain. We need you to fly the five Kyril fighters out to Area 51 and scare the Skarzi. At the very least make them think twice before launching a larger attack on planet Earth", said Gabriel, watching Paul's reaction.

Paul found the corner of the bed and sat quietly for a few seconds absorbing what Gabriel had said. There were so many things that could go wrong. The first and biggest problem was that he had never flown any type of aircraft before, let alone an Annunaki space fighter. What if the Skarzi fired at him? What if some of the Kyril spacecraft were destroyed? Martin would be furious at the loss, not to mention the loss of secrecy. Up until now, no one beyond a few select people knew of their existence. Paul pondered the situation for a few seconds, but in the end, it came down to two things: people were going to die and the Skarzi would see Earth as a pushover, inviting further attacks.

"I'll do it", said Paul with a sigh as he got up from the bed and began putting on his clothes, including his DarkWeave suit.

"Excellent. Raphael is at the cavern preparing the ships. I will be accompanying you on this mission and Raphael will be handling things at the cavern. We are limited in the aid we can give, but will do what we can to help", said Gabriel.

"I'm ready. Will I be back before Maggie wakes up?" asked Paul, as he finished dressing.

"Yes. You should be back well before then, if all goes according to plan. First though, I need to hide you from Eva. It would be best to keep your location a secret for now", said Gabriel, as he waved his hand around Paul's head.

"All set. Follow me", said Gabriel, as he waved his hand again, causing a golden, glowing gateway to appear. Gabriel stepped through, followed by Paul, who paused and took one last look at Maggie, still sound asleep. He didn't know how she would react upon finding out about this. Hopefully, he and the five spacecraft would be back all in one piece. Turning back, he stepped through the gateway and into another unknown situation.

Raphael stepped out of the shimmering, golden gateway and gazed around the dark Antarctic cavern. He closed the palm of his hand, concentrated and opened it, revealing a small, golden, glowing orb. The golden orb rose into the air, glowing brighter as it rose towards the cavern ceiling. Darkness faded away and the shadows grew smaller, as the orb brightened in intensity. The orb reached full brightness and Raphael walked over to the two cryo-sleep chambers containing the sleeping figures of Commander Kalon and his son Jalon. He checked the readouts on both chambers, verifying that all systems were within operating parameters. Satisfied that the Commander and his son were safe and in good health, Raphael turned his attention towards the five Kyril spacecraft sitting at the far end of the cavern.

Walking over to one of the fighters, Raphael looked at it wistfully, a reminder of a time long past, when he and others had been Annunaki. Sleek, jet black and diamene armored, the fighters had once been the height of Annunaki engineering. They had been a formidable weapon against the Skarzi and had helped turn the tide in many battles. These five special versions of the fighter, had been created with an added AI processor. Touching an indentation near the cockpit, Raphael was rewarded with a click, as the cockpit door swung upward, allowing him access to the interior.

"A good sign", said Raphael to himself. As he stepped up into the interior, the lights came on inside and a voice began speaking in the ancient Annunaki tongue. Raphael, already expecting to hear an Annunaki voice, understood immediately what the voice was saying.

"Please identify yourself", said the male sounding voice.

Raphael thought for a moment. With these spacecraft being literally thousands of years old, whatever information they held in memory would have to be from that time. Raphael smiled, as a long forgotten memory surfaced.

"Junior Engineer Raphael. Emergency code Adis, Kepto, Tumac", said Raphael, remembering his early years as a junior engineer.

"Greetings, Junior Engineer Raphael. I am Maruk, the AI of this spacecraft. Full access granted. How can I help you?" said the AI, Maruk.

"Hello, Maruk. I'm assigning you as the primary AI. Send the emergency code to the other four spacecraft then run a diagnostic scan of this craft and the other four spacecraft", ordered Raphael, who waited patiently for the response.

"Completed, Junior Engineer Raphael. The other four AI systems accepted the code and have returned a system status. All ships are fully functional and mission capable", replied Maruk.

"Excellent, Maruk. Have all the ships power up and ready for launch. We will be joined by two others. Gabriel and a human named Paul. You once knew him as Valinor. Once aboard, he will be in command and you will take your orders from him", ordered Raphael, pleased that the stasis field had kept the ships in perfect condition.

"Valinor? Yes, I remember. He flew this craft and the other four down from the colony ship. I remember someone else with him. Shaynor, I believe", replied Maruk.

"Yes. That is correct. Shaynor will not be joining us at this time. I must get the gateway ready. Continue getting the ships ready", said Raphael, as he left the ship.

Walking over to a far wall, he stood in front of the gateway generator, a small console capable of generating a gateway almost as large as the cavern. Raphael checked the circuits and ran some preliminary diagnostics. Satisfied with the results, Raphael entered a code linking the gateway operation to the fighter containing Maruk. Sensing a gateway forming nearby, he turned just as the gateway opened, casting a golden glow around the cavern. Gabriel stepped out, followed by Paul, the gateway closing behind them. It was time to go, thought Raphael to himself.

Chapter 11: The Assault

Commander Skresh-Ka bolted upright in his plush bed and looked down at his personal communicator. It was beeping incessantly with a message from Captain Breesh. Skresh-Ka gazed down at it through sleepy eyes focusing on the image of Captain Breesh. Tapping the communicator, the excited voice of Captain Breesh began speaking.

"Commander, we have reached Earth undetected and are in orbit above the target area. We are ready to commence the assault", said the image of Captain Breesh.

"Excellent, Captain. I will join you shortly to give the order", said Skresh-Ka as the last vestiges of sleep quickly fell away. He must've been more tired than he thought.

"Yes, Commander", replied Captain Breesh, signing off.

Skresh-Ka watched the image blank out and climbed out of bed. Still dressed in his uniform, he brushed out the rumples and headed for the door. He didn't know whether to be excited or fearful. A lot was riding on this mission and its success. Failure would certainly cause harm to both his and his family's reputations. He could even be ousted from his status as Commander. No doubt High Lord Greesh-Ka would enjoy that. He quickly made his way to the bridge, with more salutes from the ship's crew along the way.

Entering the bridge, Skresh-Ka was greeted with a flurry of activity, as preparations were being made for the assault.

"We are ready, Commander. All ships are waiting to begin the assault", said Captain Breesh, a touch of excitement in his voice.

"Good work, Captain. The Ketska will provide support for the assault force, operating in low Earth orbit. The scout ships will assist our ground troops in eliminating any ground resistance. Ground troops will follow orders given by their respective commanders. Begin the assault", commanded Skresh-Ka.

"Yes, Commander. Commencing assault", replied Captain Breesh, his reptilian eyes once again blinking with excitement.

Skresh-Ka watched the view screens as the assault operation began to unfold, his own reptilian eyes also blinking with excitement. This would be the first real battle engagement in many generations of Skarzi and hopefully their training would be up to the task, thought Skresh-Ka to himself. His other thought was that High Lord Greesh would be looking for the smallest reason to remove him from his position as Commander. Everything had to work according to plan, no exceptions. Success was the only viable outcome, as Skresk-ka settled back into his chair and watched his plan unfold.

The Ketska, in orbit above the Earth, began launching ten communications disruptors towards the target known as Area 51. The disruptors streaked towards Area 51, anti-gravity engines fired, slowing their descent dramatically. The ten disruptors spread out, equidistant from each other, encircling Area 51 with a diameter of five miles. Landing with a light thud, the disruptors began powering up their electromagnetic pulse generators. Metal rods shot into the soil beneath the disruptors, to a depth of two meters in order to create an EMP bubble, above and below the surface. With their pulse generators fully charged, the disruptors released their built up electromagnetic charge in one titanic burst, virtually frying every unshielded electronic circuit above and below ground, within the EMP bubble.

Even some shielded electronic circuits were not immune to the pulse and succumbed to its power.

Chapter 12: Retrieval

Once a brightly lit installation, Area 51 was now engulfed in total darkness. Flashes of light could be seen from base security and a contingent of Marines, as they wielded flashlights in the darkness. The Skarzi disruptors powered down their EMP generators, just as the Skarzi scout ships swooped in, firing energy weapons at vehicles and buildings. Whatever the energy beans touched, it was instantly reduced to ash or molten slag. With the scout ships cloaked and in stealth mode, they were virtually undetectable both visually and electronically. The Marines and security forces, unable to discern viable targets, were reduced to firing randomly in the hopes of hitting something. The scout ships having destroyed anything that constituted a major risk to the operation, hovered above the installation, ready to unleash more destruction. Moments later, the troop transports landed, disgorging hundreds of Skarzi warriors, wearing combat body armor, rendering them impervious to the primitive weapons wielded by the human defenders. Once emptied, the transports, still in stealth mode, rose into the air, taking positions above the Skarzi warriors.

Captain Abeesh, leader of the ground assault, signaled the Skarzi ground teams to move forward towards the installation. The assault force began taking fire from the human defenders, but were unaffected by the primitive projectile weapons. The humans turned to using laser weapons, which proved to be slightly more effective in compromising the Skarzi body armor. It was a limited effort, for once fired, the scout ships would target the laser and fire their energy weapons at the defender. The Skarzi advanced, reaching a nearby building that had been reduced to a mix of ash and molten metal. Captain Abeesh, reaching the former building, motioned for a Skarzi warrior equipped with a ground scanner, to begin scanning for tunnels. Within seconds, the warrior's scanner found a nearby tunnel, almost directly under them.

The tunnel appeared to be some 20 meters below the surface and apparently reinforced. Captain Abeesh signaled for all the ground teams to pull back a hundred yards from the tunnel location and keep the humans busy. He then contacted one of the scout ships, gave it the coordinates and retreated to a safe position, as the scout ship swooped in. Taking a position above the tunnel, the scout ship began firing its energy weapons at the spot. Within minutes, a ten foot diameter shaft had been blasted out, to a depth of twenty meters, breaching the underground tunnel. Finished with creating a shaft, the scout ship paused and began scanning the uncovered, breached tunnel. Using the gathered data, the scout ship built a database of the sub-surface installation. Scanning complete, the scout ship pulled away, returning to its previous location above the Skarzi forces. Captain Abeesh gave the shaft a couple of minutes to cool down, before advancing towards it and once there he signaled for the retrieval team to begin operations.

The retrieval team, consisting of twenty-five heavily armed Skarzi warriors, began anchoring two, light-weight, silvery ladders onto the shaft and paused before descending into the dark shaft. Team Leader Oreesh lowered his augmented visor and began descending into the shaft, followed by the rest of the team. He reached the bottom of the shaft and dropped into the tunnel, his heavy boots making a crunching sound on the floor. The rest of the team quickly followed and took up defensive positions in the wide tunnel. Their augmented visors turned the dark tunnel into almost daylight conditions. Oreesh surveyed the wide tunnel, as he pulled out his location scanner and looked for the signal that had drawn the Skarzi here. He waited, while scanning data was downloaded from one of the scout ships. A green dot began to flash on a three dimensional screen.

The signal was coming from a location a thousand yards ahead and five hundred feet below the surface. Oreesh gave directions to two warriors, ordering them to collapse the tunnel one hundred yards in the opposite direction. This would prevent any surprise attack from that direction. He and the remaining retrieval team began moving towards the signal location, wary of any counter-attack by the humans. He heard a muffled explosion from far behind them, a signal the tunnel had collapsed. The two warriors, who had collapsed the tunnel, rejoined the retrieval team, just as it reached a stairway that led downward in the direction of the signal. The team descended to a deeper level, but they still needed to descend a few more levels to reach the target.

Deeper into enemy territory the team descended until finally reaching the depth of the signal. They were now in a long corridor, with doors set on either side along its length. The signal was coming from behind a nearby door, with a strange language written on it. Suddenly, a warrior was knocked down, red blood gushing from the impact of some projectile, the deadly wound quickly closing, as the armor healed. The warrior was clearly dead, despite his armor. Oreesh couldn't believe what he saw, his reptilian eyes blinking with disbelief. Their Skarzi body armor consisted of talin, a dense, organic, self-healing compound. Impervious to projectile and most energy weapons it had been a mainstay of the Sook warrior for thousands of years. Yet here was proof that it could be compromised.

All this ran through Oreesh's mind, just as a warrior caught some movement at the far end of the corridor. Firing his energy weapon, the energy beam struck the human, reducing him to ash. Oreesh ordered the team into a defensive position, as he lowered his own energy weapon at the metal door separating the team from the signal source. He fired his weapon, the energy beam impacting the metal door and reducing it to a lump of molten slag. Oreesh looked into the room, while the slag cooled and saw a long metal cylinder sitting atop some type of wheeled conveyance. The green dot on his scanner turned a bright red, signaling him that this was the target.

Oreesh stepped over the slowly cooling thresh-old, motioning for ten of his warriors to follow. They paused just inside the room, scanning for any threats, but the room was empty. Oreesh walked over to the cylinder, large enough to hold a body and peered through a glass view port. Oreesh stepped back, stunned by what he had seen. There was a Skarzi body inside! Oreesh didn't know who it was, only that Commander Skresk-Ka wanted it. That was enough for Oreesh, who signaled four warriors to carry the cylinder. The four warriors grasped a handrail on either side with their reptilian hands and effortlessly lifted the white cylinder, while awaiting further commands. Oreesh noted that the humans probably found the cylinder heavy and cumbersome, a complete opposite to his warriors.

Oreesh directed the warriors carrying the cylinder out of the room, cautioning the warriors not to drop it. He then sent a coded message to the Ketska, informing it that they were in possession of a cylinder containing the body of a dead Skarzi and the source of the signal. Oreesh smiled at the "Well done" response from the Ketska. Now all he had to do was get it and the rest of the team out of here safely. So far they had met the most minimal of resistance, which was unexpected, as they had planned for more of a fight from these humans. He didn't know what they were planning, but he knew what he had to do.

"Let's get out of here!" ordered Oreesh to his team, as they began their journey back to the surface.

Chapter 13: Response

Deep within the depths of Cheyenne Mountain, home of NORAD, Air Force Corporal Susan Taylor sat in front of her virtual display monitoring the airspace and communications channels of Area 51. It was one of three "black sites" around the continental United States that were her responsibility. Other Air Force personnel monitored the other "black sites" including those of DarkBridge Technology. Things were normal and without incident a couple of hours into her shift, which had started at 22:00 and would end at 04:00 the next day. As soon as the clock reached 24:00 hours, things began to fall apart.

First, her systems monitoring communications with Area 51 went dead and then the infrared images of Area 51 began showing intense heat flares erupting on the surface. Something was wrong. She immediately touched the alarm button on the display, which signaled her commanding officer to come over.

"What do we have, Corporal?" asked Major Tom Ellis.

"I have a communications outage at Area 51", replied Corporal Taylor.

"Could be a power issue at the base", replied Major Ellis.

"Yes, I did consider that, but then I started seeing this", replied Corporal Taylor, as she showed the Major the thermal images from the site.

Major Ellis took one look at the thermal images and knew that the unthinkable had happened. Someone was attacking Area 51. "Activate the old fiber link with the site and scramble two recon fighters. I'll inform General Turner", replied Major Ellis. General Turner was in command of all operations at NORAD and would need to be informed.

"Thank you, Corporal. Keep me informed", said Major Ellis.

"Yes, sir", replied Corporal Taylor.

Major Ellis left the floor of the Command Center and walked up the stairs to the General's office. It was just after midnight and the light was still on in the office, but the door was closed. General Turner had a reputation for working late, often being seen walking around the Command Center at 2 o'clock in the morning. He knocked on the door to the General's office and waited for a reply.

"Who is it?" came the gruff response from the General.

"Major Ellis, sir. There's something you'll want to see", replied the Major.

"Come in, Major", replied the General.

Major Ellis opened the door and stepped into the sparsely furnished office. The General sat behind his large metal desk, reviewing hard copy reports and making notations. Major Ellis brushed off the gruffness, thinking he might be the same if he spent the same amount of time here as the General.

"Corporal Taylor is reporting some disturbing data from Area 51. If you call up Station 20, you'll see what I mean", said Major Ellis.

"Let's see what we have", replied the General, as he pushed his paperwork aside and activated the monitoring program on his terminal. Using this program, he was able to remotely monitor any of the active stations on the floor.

The screen lit up with the data from Station 20, showing the loss of communication and what looked to be heat flares appearing on what were topside buildings.

"I see what you mean. My first thought was a warfare simulation, but we would've heard beforehand. Ruling that out, it looks like there might be some sort of attack going on. What actions did you take?" asked the General.

"I had the old fiber optic link activated and scrambled two recon jets, to get a visual", replied Major Ellis.

"Those are good first steps. We need more information in order to render assistance if needed. Not much we can do until we know more. Keep me posted", said the General.

"Yes sir. We should have something soon", replied Major Ellis.

"Great job Major. You're dismissed", said the General, as he watched Major Ellis leave and focused back on the image from Area 51. Turner couldn't believe what he was seeing. Area 51 appeared to be under attack and was sustaining heavy damage. Area 51, a "black site" area, was under the command of General Robert Esterbrook. Turner knew Bob Esterbrook well, both had been classmates at the Air Force Academy and had graduated together. General Turner let out a deep sigh. It was going to be a long night.

General Robert Esterbrook had just fallen asleep in his sleeping quarters at Area 51, when he heard a chime sounding from his implant. It had been a long day touring the other "black sites" and overseeing the continued study of the alien body transported from DarkBridge. The chime was insistent and he roused himself to wakefulness. Groggy from only a couple hours of sleep, he woke to a room lit only by the dim emergency lights. He thought it odd that the emergency lights were on and tried unsuccessfully to turn on the regular lights.

"Adam. What's wrong with the lights and why are you chiming me?" said the General in a somewhat gruff voice.

"General, I have bad news to report. The base is under attack by parties unknown. There have been casualties and most of the above ground structures have been destroyed. There has also been an incursion into the lower levels. Our efforts in repelling the attack have been in vain", replied Adam, the Area 51 AI.

General Esterbrook took a few moments to digest what Adam had said. Area 51 attacked? Casualties? Bewildered, he questioned Adam again.

"Do we know who it is that's attacking us and where the lower level incursion taking place?" asked the General.

"Based on the technology being employed, I deduce, with a high probability, that it is a response to the signal emitted by the alien body. The attackers are using technology much more advanced than what we have and are most likely alien. The incursion source was from an upper level breach and the invaders have made their way down to the lower level, specifically the room containing the alien body", replied Adam.

"It would seem that the aliens are trying to retrieve the body. Rather than risk any more lives, have all base personnel retreat to safer locations. Do not engage. I think we have enough data from the body and can let them have it", ordered the General. There was no sense in risking any more lives over this.

"Yes, General. I agree. There is one more thing. The aliens employed advanced EMP devices that knocked out most communications with the outside world and most of our power sources", replied Adam.

"I'll need detailed reports on weaponry used in the attack and anything else we know about their technology. This could be a prelude to something larger, especially after they see how lacking we are in a viable response", said the General. There was no way he was getting back to sleep tonight.

"General, I am receiving a transmission on the fiber optic link from Cheyenne Mountain. They want to know our status and if we need assistance", said Adam.

"Send this message to Cheyenne Mountain. We are under attack from a superior alien race. Casualties are heavy. Send Air Force recon mission. No further action to be taken. We will handle the matter on our own", ordered the General.

"Message sent. The reply is that they understand, but will expect an explanation later", said Adam.

"Thank you, Adam. I guess I'll get dressed and see what this is all about", said the General.

"I would urge caution. The aliens are still on the surface and have yet to withdraw from the lower levels. Unfortunately, one of our security team was just killed on the lower level. He had been armed with diamene ammo and managed to kill one of the aliens before getting killed", replied Adam.

"That's all the more reason to stand down. We've lost too many people already. Let's see what this battle looks like", said the General.

"I'm receiving data from the lower levels. A gateway has opened in the corridor near the aliens and robots have emerged. There are high energy discharges taking place. It appears that the robots are engaging the aliens in combat", said Adam.

"Robots? Any idea where they came from?" asked the General.

"Unclear, they haven't identified themselves", replied Adam.

"Too many questions Adam. I need answers now and need to see how bad things are", said the General, as he pulled on his DarkWeave suit and then his combat fatigues. Next, he grabbed his combat boots, pulled them on and tied them. Standing, he grabbed a nearby flashlight and headed for the door. Once outside in the hallway he was met by two heavily armed security officers carrying their own flashlights.

"Thank you for the security detail, Adam", said the General, as the trio headed for the command bunker.

"You're welcome, General. Good luck. I'll continue monitoring the situation and provide updates", replied Adam.

"Excellent. Thank you, Adam" said the General, as he continued on his way.

Chapter 14: Assistance

Martin had gone to bed a couple hours earlier than usual. It had been a long day, mostly spent with Natasha and getting her more acquainted with the DarkBridge facility. They had started the morning having breakfast together in the cafeteria, chatting and building a deeper rapport between them. After breakfast, Natasha expressed an interest in continuing their tour of the facility.

"Can I see more of the facility?" asked Natasha.

"Of course. I'll show you a couple of the labs. Follow me.", replied Martin, who led Natasha out of the cafeteria and down a connecting hallway leading to the various labs.

He stopped in front of the Applied Materials Lab, passed the biometric scans and opened the door, ushering Natasha inside.

"This is the Applied Materials Research Department, where our DarkWeave suits are manufactured and various other materials research projects take place. It's run by Dr. Morse", said Martin, as he looked around, but didn't see him around.

"I am most impressed with the DarkWeave suits that you've developed. They seem to have numerous applications", said Natasha, growing more impressed with Martin.

"Yes. Dr. Morse and his team are doing a fantastic job here. I have someone else that I would like you to meet", said Martin, as he led Natasha out of the lab and down the hallway to another lab.

"Here is our Advanced Physics Research Department, run by Dr. Hiram Greenwood. Hiram is also our Vice President and responsible for our dimensional gateway, anti-gravity and other advanced physics technologies", said Martin with some pride. Hiram was his best friend and without him, DarkBridge Technology would probably be a much different company or possibly not even exist.

"Yes. Dr. Hiram Greenwood. I've heard a lot about him and his research", replied Natasha.

"Let's see if he's available", said Martin, as he once again passed the biometric scans and opened the door. Gesturing for Natasha to enter, Martin closed the door behind them and scanned the lab, looking for Hiram.

Martin spotted a figure hunched over a desk, entering some sort of calculations into a hovering, virtual computer screen.

"Hello, Hiram", said Martin.

Hiram jumped, his rimmed eyeglasses sliding down his nose, as he turned and looked at Martin.

"Hi, Martin. You surprised me. Who is that with you?" asked Hiram, standing up.

"Hiram, I would like to introduce Dr. Natasha Zelensky, from Area 51. Dr. Zelensky will be our liaison with them", said Martin.

"It's a pleasure to meet you, Dr. Zelensky. I've heard of your work at Area 51", said Hiram, extending his hand to Natasha.

"Hello, Dr. Greenwood. It's an honor to meet you. I'm a big fan of your research", said Natasha with a smile, as she returned Hiram's handshake.

"Thank you, Dr. Zelensky", said Hiram, clearly blushing.

"You seem to be the only one working here", observed Natasha.

"Yes. My two assistants are vacationing in Europe", replied Hiram, adjusting his eyeglasses. Natasha looked questioningly at Martin, who offered a reply.

"My daughter Pamela and her boyfriend Trent are taking some time off. The TimeBridge mission was more difficult than expected", replied Martin.

"I'd like to meet them when they return.

Especially Pamela", said Natasha with a smile.

"I think that can be arranged. Natasha and I will let you get back to work, Hiram. Try not to work too late", said Martin.

"Thank you, Martin. Nice meeting you Dr. Zelensky. I hope to see you again", said Hiram, as he sat back down at his desk.

"Please call me Natasha, Hiram. I'll be spending a lot of time around the facility", said Natasha.

"Natasha it is", replied Hiram, smiling.

Martin guided Natasha out of Hiram's lab, waving at Hiram as he left.

They'd shared dinner together once again and once again he'd escorted Natasha back to her room before returning back to his own room. He'd found it difficult at first to fall asleep, his thoughts torn between memories of Susan and thoughts of Natasha. Indeed, it was becoming increasingly difficult to maintain a purely professional relationship with her. Eventually, he'd drifted off to sleep, a sleep filled with dreams of both Susan and Natasha. His dreams were suddenly intruded upon, by an incessant beeping noise in his ear. Irritated, Martin opened his eyes to a darkened room, the beeping apparently real and coming from his implant. It was an urgent alarm from Eva.

Martin rolled onto his back, his eyes grew accustomed to the darkness as he answered Eva's alarm.

"What's wrong, Eva?" asked a grumpy Martin. He had been awakened from a dream where he and Natasha were sitting under a large maple tree having a picnic. Thrust back into reality, Martin was in a sour mood.

"I'm afraid it's bad news, Martin. Area 51 has been attacked and most of the above ground facility has been destroyed", said Eva, as she proceeded to tell Martin what Adam, the AI at Area 51 had told her.

Martin quickly sat up in bed, his mind shrugging off sleep while trying to assimilate what Eva had just said. Area 51 attacked? Alien invaders? Alien spacecraft? At least Bob was safe, thought Martin. He'd seen his share of sci-fi movies and this seemed to follow the plot of a few of them. If he didn't know better, he would've thought he was still dreaming or at least the brunt of someone's poor joke. He knew better though, Eva's programming hadn't yet advanced to that stage, so he had to accept what she said was true.

"Inform Adam that we are ready to render whatever assistance they need", said Martin, as he began getting dressed.

"Adam is requesting security forces and medical assistance. He is also reporting that five unknown fighter craft are engaging the aliens and there appear to be advanced assault robots engaging the aliens deep within the underground levels of the installation", said Eva, her quantum processors puzzled over the activity at Area 51.

"What is Paul's present location?" asked Martin, his mind immediately jumping to the discoveries at the Antarctic cavern at the mention of robots and unknown fighter aircraft.

"He was here sleeping with Maggie and then the signal from his implant faded out. I haven't been able to reconnect", replied Eva.

"Is Maggie okay", asked Martin, his mind beginning to put the pieces together.

"Maggie is asleep in bed. I can also report that Natasha is awake. Adam has been in contact with her, filling her in with all the details", said Eva.

Martin knew that with Natasha awake, it wouldn't be long before she was knocking at his door. As far as Paul was concerned, the five unknown fighter craft could only be the Kyril combat fighters stored in the Antarctic cavern, including the advanced robots seen at Area 51. Paul must have had help in bringing these elements together, possibly with the help of the angels. Martin was a little peeved that Paul hadn't cleared the operation with him first, but there probably hadn't been time given the extreme emergency.

Their alien technology secret in Antarctica may not be a secret anymore. First things first, thought Martin.

"Eva, get a support package ready for gateway travel to Area 51. Send 30 sentry robots and a few members of the security detail first, and then send Doctor Curtis, a nurse and some medical supplies. Open the gateway at a safe distance from the combat area", said Martin.

There was a brief pause, as Eva transmitted Martin's instructions to Scott and Dr. Curtis.

"All set, Martin. I've also informed Adam of our incoming assistance", replied Eva.

"Thank you, Eva", said Martin, as he finished dressing just in time to hear his door chime ring.

"That would be Natasha", said Martin.

"Correct, Martin. How did you know?" asked Eva, impressed with Martin's predictive powers.

"Educated guess", replied Martin, as he walked over to the door and paused. He took a deep breath and opened it. Natasha stood before him, smiling, but her eyes said something different. Questions lurked there, questions that Martin wasn't sure how to answer yet. Sighing, Martin closed the door behind him, fully aware of the minefield he was stepping into.

Chapter 15: An Old Trick

Paul followed Gabriel through the golden hued gateway, his mind beginning to access the memories of Valinor. In an instant, he stepped out into the Antarctic cavern, finding it well illuminated by a golden sphere floating at the top of the cavern ceiling. He sensed a humming sound coming from the Kyril spacecraft and noticed that all five had a blue light flashing inside the cockpit. Instinctively, he knew that this meant the Kyril fighters were in standby mode and ready for combat. Looking off to the side, Paul noticed Raphael working the controls of a nearby gateway generator. He remembered it from one of his many dreams of his past life as Valinor, who with the help of Shaynor, had used it to transfer large objects from the orbiting colony ship.

Turning from the gateway console, Raphael greeted the two travelers.

"Welcome, Gabriel. I see you were successful in recruiting our pilot", he said with a smile.

"Hello, Raphael. Good to see you again after so many thousands of years", said Paul, referring to the last time he'd seen Raphael in ancient Jerusalem.

"It's good to see you Paul and in good health. Thank you for joining us on this mission", said Raphael.

"I'm all in, if it saves lives", replied Paul.

"Speaking of lives, we need to know what's happening at Area 51 right now", said Gabriel, as he closed his hand, concentrated and opened it, revealing a golden orb.

"Agreed. Send it", replied Raphael. They really needed to know what the Skarzi were up to.

Gabriel opened a tiny gateway and sent the orb through, keeping the gateway open for the orb to return.

"We should know in a few minutes. In the meantime, we should prepare for departure", said Gabriel.

"I'm not sure I can fly one of these", said Paul, gesturing towards the Kyril spacecraft.

"Gabriel can help with that", said Raphael.

"Of course", said Gabriel, as he reached out and touched Paul's forehead.

Paul's mind was instantly flooded with operational knowledge of the Kyril spacecraft, instilling a level of confidence in his ability to fly one.

"The flying skills of Valinor should surface, once we're sitting inside the spacecraft", said a hopeful Gabriel.

"I hope so, but what is the tactical situation? What are we facing as far as Skarzi forces?" asked Paul.

"Gabriel and I have seen six Skarzi spacecraft depart Mars for Earth. Two troop transports, three scout ships and one battle cruiser, presumably in orbit", replied Raphael.

Paul let out a deep breath that he didn't realize he was holding. Five Kyril fighters against a significantly larger Skarzi force. It didn't sound promising and seemed like a suicide mission to him. A combat memory of Valinor popped into his mind.

"Radar spoofing", Paul blurted out.

Raphael looked at Gabriel, thinking that Gabriel had done something to Paul's mind causing some sort of psychosis.

"What's that?" inquired Gabriel, his concern for Paul skyrocketing.

"It occurred to me that the Skarzi may not be deterred by only five Kyril fighters. Then a combat memory of Valinor came to me. He once used a bunch of small drones transmitting a Kyril radar signature to fool the Skarzi. To them, it appeared that a much larger force was attacking them. The Skarzi had retreated in the face of an overwhelming force", replied Paul.

"Interesting", said Gabriel, frowning in thought.

"Yes, that might just work", replied an excited Raphael, who quickly disappeared into the lead Kyril spacecraft. Once there, he interrogated the AI, Maruk, who informed him that the five Kyril fighters were each equipped with a complement of forty small drones. Raphael smiled and reappeared outside the spacecraft.

"Good news! Each of the fighters is equipped with forty small drones that can generate a Kyril signature. We will look like a force of over two hundred fighters to the Skarzi", beamed Raphael, who hid a nagging thought that somehow this contingency had been anticipated and each fighter had been outfitted with the same number of drones. Very unusual he thought to himself. Gabriel smiled, along with Paul who now thought they had a chance of pulling this off.

Just then the golden orb returned and settled into Gabriel's outstretched palm, the gateway closing behind it. Gabriel concentrated, as the orb began downloading what it had seen. A look of worry and concern formed on his face.

"What's wrong, Gabriel?" asked Raphael.

"The Skarzi have attacked Area 51, leveling many of the above ground structures and have penetrated the tunnel system giving them access to the underground facilities. There have also been many casualties", said Gabriel, as the mood in the cavern took on a more somber tone.

Raphael digested what Gabriel had reported, realizing now that this might have to be a two pronged mission. Both an air and ground assault seemed necessary.

"My friends, it looks like we need to add a ground component to our mission. Gabriel will accompany Paul in the lead Kyril fighter and I will take a contingent of assault robots into the underground facility. Between us, we may cause the Skarzi to reconsider any future actions", said Raphael.

"I like it. What about you, Paul?" asked a curious Gabriel.

Paul thought about it. His thoughts were on the current casualties, but also realized that they needed to prevent an even larger, more deadly attack.

"Sounds like a plan. We should get moving", replied Paul.

"I'll open the gateway as soon as you're ready. Good luck", said Raphael.

"You too", replied Paul as he began walking towards the lead Kyril fighter.

"Good luck, Raphael. I'll do what I can to keep Paul safe", said Gabriel.

"I don't think Vermont Guardian would be very happy if anything happened to him", said Raphael in a lowered voice, so that only Gabriel could hear.

Gabriel nodded and waved goodbye and caught up to Paul, who was waiting patiently at the Kyril fighter.

"Ready?" asked a nervous Paul.

"Ready", replied Gabriel as he noticed Paul's nervousness.

Paul instinctively pressed his finger against a small depression on the side of the sleek, black fighter and was rewarded, as an entry hatch lifted open and a ramp extended out. Glancing inside, Paul saw that the interior was well lit and roomy considering its size. Paul walked up the ramp and headed towards the cockpit, followed by Gabriel. A disembodied voice called out to Paul.

"Hello, Paul. Hello Gabriel. Welcome aboard. My name is Maruk, the AI assigned to this spacecraft. Raphael told me to expect you. We can get underway once you're settled in", said Maruk.

"Thank you, Maruk. It's been thousands of years since I've flown, so bear with me", replied Paul, trying to inject some humor into a situation that was becoming overwhelming. Even with the Valinor memories and the knowledge boost from Gabriel, he still felt some trepidation at flying such an advanced spacecraft.

"Don't worry. I will assist if necessary", said Maruk.

"I'm here right behind you Paul, so try not to worry. You'll do fine", added Gabriel, who was right behind Paul as they made their way to the cockpit.

"Thank you both. I'll try my best", said Paul, as he settled onto the black, cushioned, pilot's chair. Paul began to get a sense of familiarity with the spacecraft, as Valinor's memories began to take over. The chair, designed for the taller Anunnaki race, instantly conformed to his body size, cushioning him against high velocity maneuvers. Paul looked at the command console in front of him, its controls labeled in the ancient Anunnaki language.

At first, it looked like some incomprehensible, flashing gibberish to him, but the longer he looked, the more familiar the writing became.

"We must hurry", said Gabriel, as he relayed a mental message to Raphael that they were ready.

Raphael, receiving the mental message from Gabriel, activated the ancient gateway generator. A small bluish rectangle appeared in front of the lead Kyril fighter, growing larger and larger, until big enough to allow safe passage of the fighters.

"Here we go", replied Paul, watching through the cockpit window as the gateway reached a safe size.

Relying on ancient Valinor memories and the memory boost from Gabriel, his fingers slid over the console, activating the anti-gravity drive. The Kyril fighter lifted a couple of feet off the ground and Paul slid his finger across the console again causing the fighter to slowly float towards the gateway. The other four Kyril fighters rose into the air, waiting their turn to move through the gateway. Paul took a deep breath, as his fighter passed into the gateway.

One by one, the remaining fighters followed him through the gateway and as the last one passed through, Raphael closed the gateway. He would re-open it when the mission was done and the fighters were returning. With Paul and Gabriel on their way, Raphael turned his attention to the assault robots. Using a nearby command console, he awakened twenty of the two hundred stored in the cavern. Using the same console, he designated one of the robots as leader and programmed some mission parameters into it. Capable of autonomous thought, the lead robot would control the operation of the other nineteen, with Raphael in ultimate control as a precaution.

Walking back to the gateway generator, he opened a smaller gateway into an underground corridor at Area 51. The familiar, bluish gateway appeared, smaller in size than the previous one, but large enough to safely pass a robot through. The lead robot turned to Raphael, who gave the signal to proceed. Receiving the signal, the lead robot began marching towards the gateway, its metal clad feet thudding against the cavern floor with every step towards the waiting gateway. Once there, the lead robot passed through it, followed by the remaining nineteen robots. Raphael watched the last robot pass through the gateway and closed it. Raphael smiled, as he opened his own personal gateway to Area 51. Everything was now in play and he hoped the Skarzi would take notice, refraining from any further action. Readying himself for the unexpected, he stepped into the gateway, closing it behind him.

Chapter 16: The Watcher

A tiny gateway opened on a bluff overlooking Area 51 and a small, black scorpion scuttled out, its tiny legs tapping across the rugged, rocky terrain. Leviathan scuttled across the rocks, seeking a good vantage point to view the activity going on at Area 51. Asmodeus had sensed some unusual energies coming from the area and was curious as to what it was. Leviathan had been in the unlucky position of being one of only two demons in the throne room at the time, with Lilith being the other. Leviathan had been the logical choice, since Lilith was still on the outs with Asmodeus and hadn't regained her full strength yet.

Leviathan found a perch upon a flat rock overlooking the base and gazed out across the flat plain below. His demon senses soon found the cause of the strange energies detected by Asmodeus. The base was under attack by what Leviathan knew to be the Skarzi. Leviathan had once been Anunnaki, like Asmodeus and had fought against the Skarzi in many battles. He thought the Skarzi had died out thousands of years ago, but here they were, as un-believable as it looked. He had mixed feelings with what he was seeing. A part of him hoped that the humans would triumph and the other part could care less. No matter, he was only here to report back to Asmodeus what he'd seen.

Glancing over the scene below and using his de-mon vision, Leviathan could see the Skarzi warriors and the Skarzi spacecraft in stealth mode. Nothing was hidden from the eyes of the demon, Leviathan. The Skarzi spacecraft, hidden from the humans and their technology, were as clear as day to Leviathan. He spotted a group of Skarzi descending into a shaft they had blasted open, but was unsure as to what they were looking for. The Skarzi had done a good job of destroying most of the surface buildings and were eliminating the human surface resistance. The humans didn't stand a chance against the superior Skarzi technology.

Leviathan, thinking this battle lost, was about to open a gateway back to Hell, when suddenly, he was knocked off his perch by a rush of air. Cursing, he scrambled back onto his rocky perch to see what had knocked him off. Shock came over him as he saw something that shouldn't be here, something that hadn't existed for thousands of years. His scorpion eyes stared in disbelief, as he recognized the strange objects. They were Kyril fighters, the most advanced spacecraft the ancient Anunnaki had ever developed. Leviathan was at a loss to explain what he was seeing. The spacecraft weren't even in stealth mode, as if they wanted to be seen. Leviathan concentrated, augmenting his senses on the lead fighter and came away shocked. The lead Kyril fighter held the angel Gabriel and the human called Paul Cross, who had once been known as Valinor. It began to make some sense to Leviathan, having Valinor, the best combat pilot in the Anunnaki fleet, flying the Kyril fighters against the Skarzi here.

Whatever the plan was, it seemed to be having an effect on the Skarzi, who seemed to be in panic mode. Leviathan sensed something else, something deadly, a battle cruiser in orbit above the Earth. Not only that, but there were two hundred smaller objects headed towards it. Drones, he immediately thought. They had been used effectively by the ancient Anunnaki against the Skarzi in many battles, simulating a much larger force. Leviathan secretly hoped that the Skarzi had forgotten their ancient past. Evidently, they had. The orbiting battle cruiser began powering up its massive engines in an attempt to flee the false threat. Leviathan laughed at the fleeing Skarzi and could hardly contain himself. They were still falling for the old Valinor tactics.

Subduing his laughter, Leviathan turned his attention back to the drama unfolding below him, as the five real Kyril fighters swooped down and began firing their energy weapons at the Skarzi. The five fighters seemed to be working in unison as if linked together. Leviathan adjusted his demon senses and could see a thin line connecting the five fighters. They were linked and under control of the lead fighter, presumably the one flown by the human called Paul. Leviathan watched as the Kyril energy weapons lashed at Skarzi spacecraft and Skarzi warriors alike. Scout ships fell flaming from the sky, one troop transport was completely destroyed and Skarzi ground forces were falling fast, from the advanced Kyril weapons. However curious Leviathan was of the outcome, he'd seen enough and needed to report back to Asmodeus, who might not take this news very well. Old wounds could be reopened. Reluctantly, Leviathan opened a gateway back to Hell and scuttled through with a sense of wariness and fear.

Asmodeus sat on his Throne of Fire, gone was his typical white suit, as he opted for a more demon-like appearance. His claws raked the arms of his throne, tongues of flames leaping from the gouged surface. He was still agitated with Lilith for having failed to keep Valinor and Shaynor in the past. Her defense had intrigued him, it being an astonishing tale. That she was telling the truth was somewhat evident, given her current reduced energy state. She had regained some of her energy and now was a ghostly wisp of the beauty she had once been, but it would take a bit longer for her to get back to normal. Asmodeus was puzzled by the energy being that had gone by the name of Black. There was no recorded history of Black and it seemed to just disappear from this world after the Lilith interaction.

"My Love, I find your explanation of failure intriguing and will withhold any more punishment for now", said Asmodeus to the ghost-like form of Lilith, who wavered before him.

"Thank you, my King", whispered Lilith.

Just then, a tiny gateway opened and Leviathan scuttled out.

"Welcome back, Leviathan. I fail to see why you prefer such a form to take. A scorpion just doesn't seem to instill fear in most humans, including most demons", said Asmodeus.

"It suits me, my King. It's an unassuming disguise. Besides, I have MAJOR news", replied Leviathan, emphasizing the word "major".

Asmodeus looked at Leviathan skeptically. He'd learned to take much of what his demons reported with a grain of salt.

"Alright, tell me of your "MAJOR" news" replied Asmodeus sarcastically.

Leviathan began relating what had caused the strange energy readings that Asmodeus had detected.

Asmodeus listened with growing anger, flames beginning to sprout from the back of his throne, flaming sparks coming from his raking claws.

Leviathan was glad that Lilith was there to bear some of their King's anger.

Asmodeus leaped out of his chair at the mention of the Kyril fighters, landing directly in front of Leviathan, who cowered in subservience.

"Are you sure about what you saw", said a seething Asmodeus.

"Yes, my King. There was no doubt", replied Leviathan.

Anger burned within Asmodeus as he remembered the Rebellion and how he and his fellow rebels had lacked the more sophisticated weapons that would've made the Rebellion a success.

It wasn't just the Kyril fighters though. There had been rumors circulating around the colony ship about a missing contingent of assault robots. Kyril fighters and assault robots were exactly what had been needed for the Rebellion. Someone had deliberately kept their existence hidden and a secret from everyone. Valinor, Gabriel, Raphael and possibly even Shaynor must have been in on the secret. Asmodeus was glad that Valinor and Shaynor had been killed in the command center back then, even though they had apparently been reincarnated many times since then. Asmodeus slowly let go of his anger, thinking that it really didn't matter now. He was magnitudes more powerful as a demon now than he ever would've been as Annunaki.

"Well done, Leviathan. The Skarzi and human conflict will serve us. It keeps the angels busy and offers another opportunity to kill Valinor. You may go", said Asmodeus, whose anger faded, replaced with a feeling of optimism.

"Thank you, my King", said Leviathan as he opened a gateway and disappeared.

Lilith had watched the whole episode with fear, thinking that Asmodeus would take out his anger on her. Fortunately, he seemed to have forgotten about her and his anger had subsided.

Asmodeus strode back to his Throne of Fire, sprinting up to his Throne and taking a seat once again. The flames died out behind the throne, as Asmodeus calmed down. He pondered this new wrinkle to his plans of ruling mankind and began formulating a new plan to eliminate Valinor. It came to him almost immediately, a new trap to catch Valinor, but this time he'd use the Skarzi. He'd have to act quickly though, before the opportunity passed.

"I'm sorry, my love. I need to address an issue that has just come up. I'll return soon and pick up where we left off", said Asmodeus with a sly grin, as he stood, opened a gateway and walked through.

Lilith watched Asmodeus depart, relieved with the respite from his interrogation, but at the same time fearful of her future here in Hell. Maybe he would get over her failure, which was just wishful thinking on her part. Asmodeus could be pleasant and however seemingly improbable, loving at times. The other side of the Demon King was his tendency towards anger and cruelty. Lilith walked a fine line with Asmodeus and she knew that her failure had tipped her over to his less than desirable self. She let out a heavy sigh, upon leaving the throne room, her wispy form drifting out the huge, black obsidian doors.

Chapter 17: Birds of Prey

Paul exited the gateway into a black moonless sky and increased speed on the Kyril fighter to Mach 3. He briefly thought about the sonic boom that would follow, but realized that the unique aerodynamics of the Kyril fighters would reduce that to a low thump. People on the ground would hear it as a car door closing. The four other Kyril fighters followed behind him, fanning out into a "V" shaped formation, while increasing speed to match him. Gabriel sat beside him, seemingly lost in thought.

"Maruk, please engage stealth mode on all fighters. What is our location?" asked Paul.

"Stealth mode enabled. We are east of what is known as Salt Lake City, which is passing below us, as I speak. I am monitoring various primitive aircraft flying nearby and adjusting course to avoid", replied Maruk.

"Thank you, Maruk", said Paul, as he glanced at the tactical display screen. He saw the five Kyril fighters displayed as green icons and a variety of other icons highlighted in red. They were most probably commercial passenger aircraft. Far off to the left of the screen, heading in from the west, were two icons flashing red.

"Maruk, what are those two aircraft on the far left of the display?" asked Paul.

"Those appear to be primitive fighter aircraft headed towards our target destination. Possibly a reconnaissance flight", replied Maruk.

"How soon before they get here?" asked Gabriel.

"The fighter aircraft will be here in 20 minutes. They appear to flying slower over populated areas to reduce any chance of a sonic boom.", replied Maruk.

"Not much time. It'll be close. How soon to target?" asked Paul.

"We are crossing into what is called Nevada. Time to target is three minutes", replied Maruk.

"Let me know when we're one minute out", said Paul.

"Understood", replied Maruk.

Paul nervously waited as the seconds ticked by, what was coming next would require every bit of Valinor knowledge he could recall.

"One minute out", replied Maruk.

"Disengage stealth mode, all fighters. Launch drones towards battle cruiser", ordered Paul, as he decreased the Kyril fighter's speed and dropped altitude down to three thousand feet.

Maruk disengaged stealth mode and began deploying drones from the five Kyril fighters. One by one, the drones began exiting the fighters, gathering at a point above the fighters until all two hundred drones had assembled. Once assembled, the drones began their ascent towards the battle cruiser in orbit above the Earth.

"Low and slow", said Paul, as he slowed the fighter even more and dropped in altitude, just clearing the rocky hills surrounding Area 51.

"There's a demon watching from the hill. It appears to be Leviathan", said Gabriel, in a matter of fact tone.

"Wonder what it wants?" asked Paul.

"Allow me", said Gabriel, as he used his own control console to decrease their altitude further, causing the Kyril fighters to skim the top of the hill, toppling the demon from its perch. Gabriel heard Leviathan curse, which brought a huge smile to his face, before relinquishing control back to Paul.

Paul, realizing the need for the Skarzi to recognize them as Anunnaki, made every effort to make it happen. From coming out of stealth mode to flying low and slow, he hoped it helped. What made him gasp when he looked at his view screen was the devastation wreaked upon Area 51. Buildings were burning, some turned to ash or molten slag, defender bodies littering the areas around the buildings. Paul looked at Gabriel, who had a pained expression on his face. Paul understood the angel's rule of preserving life and not interfering, so he didn't expect approval from Gabriel as the Kyril fighters swooped in to exact retribution. Like birds of prey, the Kyril fighters began targeting the Skarzi scout ships with withering fire from their energy weapons.

The scout ships were still visible to the advanced targeting systems of the Kyril fighters, despite their attempts to hide via stealth mode. The first Skarzi scout ship erupted in flames and then exploded, as the Kyril weapons sliced through its hull, piercing any protective screens and armor. The second Skarzi scout ship attempted to engage the Kyril fighters but it too, fell to the advanced Anunnaki weaponry. The third scout ship, realizing the futility of fighting, turned and began a rapid ascent into orbit. Paul turned his attention to the Skarzi warriors below and began systematically vaporizing them group by group.

Paul was about to vaporize a group coming out of what looked like an excavated shaft entrance, when Gabriel stayed his hand.

"Stop firing. There are three humans among the group. Probably being used as human shields and insurance that they won't be attacked", said Gabriel, aghast at the death and destruction he was seeing.

Paul ceased his attack and pulled away to a safe distance, his view screen zooming in on the human hostages. Two of the three were unfamiliar to him, but were dressed as base security. The third individual he knew well and made him sit back in shock.

"Crap", Paul said aloud.

"What's wrong, Paul", asked a concerned Gabriel.

"One of the hostages is General Esterbrook", replied a shocked Paul.

Gabriel looked at his friend and saw the pain etched on his face.

Paul watched the Skarzi warriors lead the prisoners into one of the troop transports and watched helplessly as it lifted into the sky. Paul couldn't take a chance on accidently destroying the transport, so he sent the Kyril fighters towards the other troop transport, which was only partly full as it began rising off the ground. Energy weapons flashing, the Kyril weapons sliced through the armored hull of the transport, triggering a massive explosion and sending the burning transport crashing to the ground. As Paul and Gabriel watched, the transport carrying the General rapidly climbed into orbit above the Earth. The transport followed behind the remaining scout ship and both accelerated in order to catch up to the escaping battle cruiser.

Paul, along with the other four Kyril fighters hovered over Area 51, making sure that the Skarzi threat was over for now. Lost in thought, Paul sat in silence, contemplating the destruction and the capture of General Esterbrook.

"It would appear that Skarzi technology hasn't progressed much over the past few thousand years. I expected our weapons to be much less effective against their ships", said Gabriel, attempting to break the silence.

"Yes, I thought we would have more trouble. Maruk, recall the drones", ordered Paul, as he and the other four ships rose to higher altitude to recover the drones. A couple of minutes later, the drones came swooping in, returning to each Kyril fighter.

"Don't worry, Paul. We'll find a way to get the General and the other two humans back", offered Gabriel.

"Thank you, Gabriel. Right now, we have to get back to the cavern", replied Paul.

"Recon aircraft 1 minute out", said Maruk.

"Maruk, engage stealth mode and take us back to the gateway coordinates", said Gabriel.

"Understood", replied Maruk, as the five Kyril fighters engaged stealth mode and headed away at top speed towards the gateway coordinates.

Chapter 18: A Devious Plan

Asmodeus had hastily stepped out into the underground corridors of Area 51 in order to implement his plan. It wasn't his first visit there, as he'd been there a few times before, keeping track of human progress. The humans had managed to capture technology from other star-faring races that had either crashed on Earth or had been captured. They had managed to reverse engineer some of this advanced technology, but it was still far behind that of the Anunnaki. Arrayed along the underground corridors were various labs containing the recovered technology and he saw one such lab with its doors melted down, allowing access to the interior. Obviously, the Skarzi had been here and had recovered something. Asmodeus had hatched a simple plan to ensnare Valinor, but it required both humans and Skarzi to make it happen.

Casting his mind out, he located the Skarzi intruders and a group of three humans inadvertently approaching the Skarzi. "Perfect", said Asmodeus to himself, as he opened another gateway nearby the Skarzi intruders and stepped through. He exited the gateway and found the nearby Skarzi, slowly making their way back to the surface. They appeared to be carrying a long, metallic cylinder, which was probably their reason for coming here and important to them. Intrigued, Asmodeus went over for a closer look, invisible to the Skarzi warriors. Peering inside the cylinder, Asmodeus saw the remains of a long dead Skarzi. From the robe it still wore, Asmodeus determined that the fabric was ancient Hebrew and there was a bullet hole that had easily passed through the talin, self-healing armor it wore underneath. Only a diamene bullet could do that and it was one more piece of evidence that was leading him to one conclusion.

"Could it be from the time of Solomon? Could the Skarzi have been there at the same time as Valinor? thought Asmodeus, still preferring to use the Valinor name, despite the numerous reincarnations. Questions swirled in his mind, as he thought about the implications. Maybe Lilith's journey hadn't been a failure after all. The more he thought about it, the more it made sense. Paul and his team, traveling to the past, had encountered the Skarzi and killed at least one. It was irrelevant as to how the body arrived here at this time period. The important thing was that it had brought the attention of the Skarzi to Earth and enough attention to destroy the base above.

This was too good to be true, thought Asmodeus. Here was a Skarzi body from three thousand years ago, drawing the Skarzi here and ironically causing Valinor to get involved personally in defending the base. Asmodeus smiled, now all he had to do was prime the trap. Locating the leader of the Skarzi group, Asmodeus floated over to him and placed a simple, driving thought in its mind, "Get hostages".

That being done, Asmodeus turned his attention towards the humans and made his way over to them. Here he placed an aura of confusion around the three humans, one of which seemed to be of high military rank. Asmodeus then sent them hurrying towards the waiting Skarzi and watched with satisfaction, as the Skarzi leader set his weapon to stun and fired at the humans. The humans went down in a heap and were roughly gathered up by the Skarzi. Asmodeus smiled. The trap was now baited and he had no doubt that Valinor would attempt a rescue. It was now Valinor against the Skarzi Empire. Asmodeus laughed, satisfied with the deviousness of his plan, as he opened a gateway back to Hell and stepped through.

The two recon fighters, engines screaming, approached Area 51, from the west, slowing to cruising speed and dropping to low altitude as they started a preliminary pass over the site.

"Whiskey, Tango, Alpha. Recon 1 over target now", reported the lead fighter.

"Roger, Whiskey, Tango, Alpha. Report damage assessment and signs of alien attackers", responded General Turner at NORAD.

"Whiskey, Tango Alpha. No sign of alien attackers. Signs of destroyed spacecraft, ground buildings destroyed. Cameras enabled, turning for another pass", replied the Recon 1 fighter.

"Whiskey, Tango, Alpha. Request confirmation of alien presence", replied General Turner.

"Whiskey, Tango, Alpha. Confirmed. No sign of alien attackers. Site is clear. Repeat. Site is clear. Survivors spotted and triage tents deployed", replied the Recon 1 fighter.

"Roger, Whiskey, Tango, Alpha. Complete damage assessment and return to base. NORAD out", replied General Turner.

"Whiskey, Tango, Alpha, Roger. Completing assessment and returning to base", replied the Recon 1 fighter.

General Turner at back in his chair assessing what Recon 1 had just reported. The aliens were gone, having completed whatever mission they had come to Earth for. There would be a ground assessment, but that would fall under Bob Esterbrook's command. Turner had done his part and it was now up to higher levels on a course of action. Turner glanced at the blue phone, knowing that the people on the other end would know far more about the situation. Further instructions would have to come from them. He fervently hoped that this attack wasn't a prelude to something larger. It was turning into a long night and it still wasn't over. A report had just come in about a Russian drone incursion over Alaska. Sighing, Turner got back to work.

Chapter 19: Captured

Team leader Oreesh sat in the troop transport looking down at the three humans on the floor in front of him. Clearly they were an inferior species that many Skarzi considered little more than vermin. Oreesh didn't have an opinion one way or another, being a warrior he looked at threat potential more than anything else. The three humans lying on the metal floor, in his estimation posed little threat to the Skarzi. He'd heard multiple rumors, one being that human specimens had been captured and taken back to Mars at various times over the past three thousand years, specifically for testing and experimentation.

He'd also heard a more disgusting and revolting rumor that some Skarzi considered them a delicacy. That rumor had included a mention of his superior,

Captain Abeesh, who reportedly was involved along with others in smuggling humans in from Earth to feed their unsavory appetites. Looking at the humans, Oreesh couldn't fathom eating one, his head turning away from the captives in disgust. Having been raised from a hatchling to be a Sook warrior, he'd learned to look the other way when it came to questioning his superiors, which suited his plans for advancement. His mind drifted back to the dramatic turn of events that now had the three humans lying stunned in front of him.

It had been a necessity to capture them as events on the surface took an unexpected turn for the worse. Below the surface, the team had successfully recovered the artifact, but had lost two warriors to a human sniper. Then, the team found itself harried, unbelievably, by a group of Anunnaki assault robots. Oreesh, finding his team faced with death above and below, made a tactical decision to capture some human prisoners to be used as shields and maybe as a deterrent from attack on the surface. That decision had suddenly coalesced in his mind almost instantly. At the time Oreesh was too busy to wonder at it, but now he found it very unnerving.

The team had fled from the Anunnaki robots, encountering the three humans attempting to reach some sort of secure area. Oreesh had switched his energy weapon to stun and fired at the humans, who fell to the ground unconscious. At his command, they were scooped up by three hulking Skarzi warriors, each easily slinging a human across its back. Oreesh and his team, carrying their three insurance policies and the artifact, reached the shaft and climbed back up to the surface. Once on the surface, Oreesh had blinked his reptilian eyes in disbelief, as he gazed upon the devastated Skarzi assault force. One scout ship was fleeing into orbit and two others destroyed. The Skarzi mastery of the battlefield had turned into disaster.

"Head towards the nearest transport", sounded the voice of Captain Abeesh over the communications channel.

Oreesh remembered looking over at the nearest transport and seeing Captain Abeesh waving from the ramp. Seeing the Captain, Oreesh complied and led his team towards the transport. They boarded it in record time, joining Captain Abeesh and ten other warriors. From the transport, Oreesh had watched as five dark shapes swooped in and fired upon the other troop transport, energy weapons slicing through the Skarzi armor. He had watched with dismay, as the transport erupted in flames and exploded. The crew and warrior teams incinerated. Remarkably, the five fighter craft held off on firing at his troop transport, probably because of the hostages. A snap decision had probably saved his life and that of his team. The ramp closed and Oreesh, weary from the assault, sat heavily upon the padded seat, his human captives spread out before him.

Oreesh, waking from his musings, blinked his reptilian eyes and noticed one of the humans starting to stir. Pulling up his energy weapon, he fired a brief stun pulse, sending the human back into unconsciousness. Keeping a keen eye on his captives, he settled into his seat, hoping that the trip back to Mars would be quick and safe. After what he had witnessed on Earth, he held little hope for the latter. Obviously, someone was aiding the humans and using technology beyond that of the Skarzi. If the humans had this level of technology, then the Skarzi intelligence gathering had failed, putting the entire mission in jeopardy. Someone would be held accountable, but it wouldn't be Oreesh. After all, he was just a Sook warrior following orders. It was going to be a long journey home after all, he thought to himself, as he settled deeper into his seat.

Chapter 20:
Reversal

Commander Skresh-Ka sat in his chair on the bridge of the Ketska, smiling wide and showing his reptilian teeth. He was basking in the good news from the assault team and the retrieval of the artifact. The assault force had met with mostly ineffective resistance from the humans, which had quickly been eliminated by the superior technology and efforts of the Skarzi forces. High Lord Greesh-Ka would be beside himself with envy, thought the ebullient Skresh-Ka.

"Congratulations, Commander. You have a glorious victory over the humans and a successful retrieval to add to your honors", said Captain Breesh.

"Thank you, Captain and thanks to all members of the assault force. They have demonstrated Skarzi superiority and have brought great honor upon their clan", said a beaming Skresh-Ka.

"Thank you, Commander", replied Captain Breesh, his own reptilian face echoing a similar smile.

"Captain Breesh, recall the", Skresh-Ka couldn't complete his order, for just as he was about to give it, klaxons began to sound and the bridge lighting turned red.

Skresh-Ka jumped up out of his seat, almost losing control of his bodily functions.

"Captain, what's wrong?" asked a stunned Skresh-Ka.

"Commander, this is going to sound unbelievable, but there are two hundred Anunnaki spacecraft approaching us from the surface. The Ketska AI has identified them as Kyril class space fighters. Also, our assault force on the surface is under attack by five Kyril fighters", reported a mystified Captain Breesh.

Skresh-Ka couldn't believe reptilian ears and quickly sat down as he tried assimilating what the Captain had just said. It couldn't be the Anunnaki? Could it be them after all this time?

No sooner had he sat down, when Captain Breesh delivered more bad news.

"Commander, we are receiving reports from the surface. Our losses are beginning to mount. One transport is lost with a full crew and partial compliment of warriors. Two scout ships with full crews are also lost ", said Captain Breesh,

Skresh-Ka sat there stunned. All eyes on the bridge seemed focused on him, looking for decisive action. Seconds ticked by, as Skresh-Ka pondered the potential fallout of his failure. High Lord Greesh-Ka would probably demote him and send him down to the hatchery to train young hatchlings. A resigned Skresh-Ka suddenly became fearful, as he recalled what Captain Breesh had said. Anunnaki! They were on their way to attack the Ketska! His flagship! Losing the Ketska would only add insult to injury, not to mention his life. He seriously doubted that High Lord Greesh-Ka would heap many honors upon him, should he die. No artifact was worth losing his life and his flagship. There was only one thing to do.

"Captain Breesh, full speed back to Mars. Put some distance between us and the attackers", ordered Skresh-Ka.

"Yes Commander. What about the assault force?" asked a concerned Captain Breesh.

"The assault force will rendezvous with us once the Ketska is safe. With human hostages onboard, the transport should be safe. As for the remaining scout ship, have it shadow the transport from a safe distance", said Skresh-Ka, feeling relieved at coming to a decision.

"Yes Commander", replied Captain Breesh, who wasn't completely comfortable with leaving the transport and scout ship on their own. The decision bordered on self-preservation and Captain Breesh wasn't sure how it would be received among the assault force. Being a good warrior, he gave the order. He was after all, just following orders.

General Robert Esterbrook felt the cold metal floor against his face. He was lying on his side and beginning to regain consciousness. His thoughts were initially confused, as he sensed some G-force acceleration taking place. Having been a fighter pilot early in his career, he was familiar with the sensation. The last thing he remembered was walking to the command center with his armed escort. They had somehow become confused in passageways that all of them were very familiar with and had traveled many times. In their confusion, they had encountered a group of unknown alien beings. One of the aliens had leveled some sort of weapon at them and fired. The effect had been immediate, rendering him and his escorts unconscious. With the weapon's effects wearing off, he noticed an unfamiliar smell in the air. The only thing he could compare it to was a cross between rotten meat and a musky odor.

He slowly lifted one eyelid, the one on the side of his face against the metal floor and took a brief look. It was all he needed to verify that he and his two escorts had been captured. He quickly closed his eye, having seen the heavy boots worn by his captors. They were unlike any boots he had ever seen and were definitely alien. Everything added up to them being hostages. Coupling everything that had happened with the signal sent from the alien corpse, he had no doubt that they were headed to Mars. What would happen there, he didn't know, but it probably wouldn't be good for either him or his men.

Any kind of rescue attempt was out of the question. Earth hadn't yet advanced to the level of interplanetary travel that these aliens had obviously achieved. Even if Earth did manage some sort of rescue attempt, it would be months before a spacecraft reached them, assuming it wasn't destroyed along the way. There was really only one person who had any chance of saving him and his men, Martin Weaver. He knew Martin well and despite some disagreements over the years, they were still very good friends. Once Martin learned about this, every attempt would be made to rescue them. A smile formed on his face, but it was a big mistake, as he felt an energy blast send him back into unconsciousness. His last brief thought, was of his son Scott and how he would take it.

Chapter 21: Bad News

Martin stood in the doorway of his apartment, his face echoing the concern showing on Natasha's face.

"Area 51 has been attacked by an unknown alien race", blurted out Natasha.

"Eva updated me on the situation and I've started dispatching personnel and supplies to the facility. I'm sorry Natasha. There are many casualties, possibly some you knew", replied Martin.

"Thank you, Martin. It probably would've been worse, but for the intervention of a small force of spacecraft that attacked the invaders and destroyed many of their spacecraft", said Natasha.

"Small force of spacecraft?" questioned Martin.

"Yes. Five spacecraft suddenly swooped in and began engaging the invaders", replied Natasha, her eyes searching Martin's face for any sign of involvement. She found none. Martin would've made a good poker player.

Martin stood there trying to think of why that number five might mean something and the fact that it was another type of alien spacecraft. Suddenly, it dawned on him as to why it meant something. The Antarctic cavern and the Anunnaki spacecraft Paul had found. Martin hid the revelation from showing on his face and was helped by a sudden tilting of Natasha's head as she received a message from Adam.

Natasha's face went ashen as she received the news. Simultaneously, Eva spoke to Martin through his implant.

"Martin, there's more bad news from Area 51. General Esterbrook and two security guards have been taken hostage by the alien invaders", said Eva.

Martin met Natasha's eyes, both of them feeling the same sense of shock.

"I'm sorry Natasha. Eva just relayed the news to me about General Esterbrook", said Martin.

"This is all too much to process, Martin. First, Area 51 is attacked and now the General is missing. Why have they taken him? How can we possibly get him back? I think he's lost to us Martin. We don't have the capability to rescue him, not to mention an adequate defense against attack. They hold the military advantage and are technologically superior to us. I just don't see any way to rescue him", said an emotional Natasha.

"Yes, it does appear impossible, but here at Dark-Bridge, we've often turned the impossible into possible. Let's go to the conference room in my office and brainstorm with my team", offered Martin.

"Okay, but I don't know how you can possibly rescue them", said a resigned Natasha.

"Eva, contact Scott, Hiram, Paul, Maggie and Dr. Morse. Tell them it's an emergency and to meet me in my conference room in a half hour. Have plenty of donuts and coffee ready", said Martin.

"I'll take care of it, Martin. I'm sorry to hear about the General. Adam and I are in close contact and agree with Natasha on how impossible a rescue would be", replied Eva.

"Thank you, Eva. Hopefully, this meeting will give us some hope", said Martin, while smiling at Natasha. Closing the door to his apartment behind him, Martin gestured for Natasha to follow him. Natasha fell in alongside Martin, unsure as to what Martin could possibly do. It seemed a futile meeting, but there was something in Martin's eyes that gave her hope.

Paul stepped out of the gateway and into his still darkened room. Gabriel had opened the gateway for him, but had decided to remain with Raphael to discuss the recent events. Paul had left Area 51 with the four other Kyril fighters flying behind him in close formation, with all five spacecraft in stealth mode. He returned to the earlier gateway coordinates that they had first exited from and found the gateway in the distance, open and waiting. Slowing his speed dramatically, almost to a crawl, his and the other four Kyril spacecraft slowly entered the gateway and exited into the Antarctic cavern without incident. Paul was still in shock about the General being taken hostage, but managed to thank Gabriel and Raphael for their help.

Now he stood back in his apartment, which was cloaked in darkness. He heard Maggie, still sleeping soundly and a sense of relief washed over him. At least she had slept through the whole incident, he thought to himself. What happened after she found out was another matter. Stripping down to his underwear, he climbed back into bed, careful not to disturb Maggie. Martin would also find out, if he hadn't already. He hoped he'd done the right thing in going, but there was a nagging thought that maybe his actions had caused the General to be taken hostage. Exhausted, he fell asleep, his dreams filled with visions of battles fought as Valinor and his most recent battle at Area 51.

Chapter 22: Coming Clean

Paul shifted in bed. He'd fallen asleep as soon as he hit the pillow, exhaustion having taken over. Ensconced in the world of dreams, an annoying beeping began sounding from his implant. Groggily, he rolled over in bed, hoping that the annoying sound would go away. It was insistent though and he reluctantly responded to its call.

"What is it Eva?" said a sleepy Paul.

"Sorry to wake you Paul. An emergency has come up at Area 51 and Martin has called an immediate meeting and would like you and Maggie to attend. By the way, you disappeared from my sensors earlier. Where did you go?" asked Eva.

Paul knew he was treading on dangerous ground here and needed a good alibi, since he wasn't yet ready to acknowledge his involvement.

"Gabriel needed my help on a special project, so I had to leave for a bit. Tell Martin that Maggie and I will be there shortly", said Paul, as he glanced over at Maggie and saw her begin to stir. He turned his head towards the clock on his nightstand and groaned at the time. It was only 3am. Climbing out of bed, he began getting ready, resigning himself to only having a couple hours of sleep. The bed shifted as Maggie sat up.

"What time is it? Eva just told me about the meeting. Did you sleep well?" asked a sleepy Maggie.

"Sorry my love, it's only 3am. No, I didn't get much sleep. There's something you should know", said Paul, making the decision to be upfront with Maggie.

"What is it?" asked a curious Maggie.

"Gabriel showed up just after we went to bed", said Paul and he launched into an abbreviated explanation of what happened.

Maggie listened intently, her eyes growing wide as Paul recounted his adventure. When he finished, the two of them sat there briefly in silence, until Maggie spoke.

"You did what you had to do, given the situation. You're my hero and I love you. The only question I have is why I never noticed you leave?" said Maggie with a questioning look.

"That would be Gabriel. He didn't want to disturb you, so he put you into a deep sleep. You aren't mad at me?" asked Paul.

"Not with you. Were I you, I would've done the same. It's Gabriel that I have a problem with", said a frustrated Maggie.

"Thank you for understanding. I wanted you to hear it from me. We need to keep this a secret between us, since no one knows", said a relieved Paul.

"You're welcome. Martin will probably put two and two together. Not much escapes him", said Maggie, a smile forming on her face.

"Speaking of Martin, he'll be waiting for us", said Paul.

"Give me 15 minutes", said Maggie, as she climbed out of bed and began getting ready.

Minutes later Maggie was ready, impressing Paul with how beautiful she looked considering what time it was.

"Shall we go?" asked a smiling Maggie.

"Absolutely!" replied Paul, ushering her towards the door. They left the apartment, walking side by side towards Martin's office, with Paul in a somewhat pensive mood. There was still a need to keep the cavern and its contents secret, especially with Commander Kalon and his son there. He hoped that Martin felt the same way. Turning to Maggie, he smiled and saw her smile back at him, as they continued walking.

Deep below the DarkBridge facility, in its sub-terranean cavern, Vermont Guardian watched the events taking place in the world above. It and the other Guardians had seen much death and destruction during the time humans had populated the Earth. Humans killing other humans, destroying each other's cities and enslaving other humans, it was all so disappointing to Vermont and the other Guardians. It was a disease waiting for a cure. Now, that death and destruction was amplified by the alien Skarzi who had had rekindled ancient hostilities and threatened the solar system with war. Distressing and disappointing, mused Vermont, as it continued thinking about the recent conflict.

The Skarzi held the upper hand with their advanced technology and left unchecked would annihilate most of the Earth's population. Any survivors would be enslaved, or worse, become a food source for hungry Skarzi warriors. The humans had little chance, given the current state of technology, but there was a glimmer of hope. In looking at the possible futures, Vermont had seen a wild card existing in the Antarctic cavern: the two Annunaki in cryosleep, held the key to Earth's salvation. However, it would be some time before that key would be used, since there were still events that needed to take place.

One event stood out from the rest of those futures, causing great concern among the Guardians. It was the eventual return of the entity known as Black. Vermont and the other Guardians were wary of Black returning, since those possible futures had shown a much more powerful Black and a danger to the Guardians. Vermont had tried to see what that danger was, but for some reason that specific event was shrouded in fog, as if someone wanted it to remain unclear. Most unsettling, Vermont thought, as it resumed monitoring the human and Skarzi conflict.

Chapter 23: Captives

Commander Skresh-Ka sat in his personal shuttle craft, watching the view screen in front of him and the receding image of the Ketska. He'd left the battle cruiser in order to resume his duties on Mars and address any questions regarding his decisions about the assault. He was still somewhat stunned by the turn of events, his glorious victory was being compared to the ancient Great Rout. Not a good comparison when your reputation is at stake. Wistfully, he watched the Ketska as it picked up speed and headed towards the Asteroid Belt to join its sister ships. He missed the Ketska already, being so far removed from the politics on Mars. He had no doubt that he would be summoned before the High Council, High Lord Greesh-Ka among them. Hissing silently, his reptilian eyes blinked in frustration as he settled deeper into his chair and continued watching the view screen.

The angry, red visage of Mars soon replaced the Ketska, now just a bright dot on the edge of the view screen. The shuttle dipped into the upper atmosphere, beginning its descent to the surface. Following close behind were the remaining scout ship and troop transport. They were all that remained of the original assault force. If he were judged solely on achieving the objective of retrieving the artifact, then the mission was a success. However, knowing High Lord Greesh-Ka, Skresh-Ka suspected that this would go badly for him.

He'd lost too many resources in the assault and would be blamed for the loss. How could he have known the Annunaki would suddenly appear? Who could've predicted that? How could the High Council fault him for something that no one could foresee? Wasn't it widely accepted that the Anunnaki were long dead? Skresh-Ka pondered these questions, as the shuttle slowed over the dusty, red Martian landscape. Diving into a deep ravine, the shuttle slowed to a hover, the ravine walls towering on each side. A massive section of the ravine wall began to slide open, revealing an even more massive interior. The shuttle maneuvered into the massive hangar, landing in its reserved location. The scout ship and troop transport landed close by, the massive hangar doors closing behind them.

Skresh-Ka stood and exited the shuttle, standing outside as the troop transport began discharging its personnel. Skresh-Ka saw the artifact, or at least something covered, being carried off by four Sook warriors. It would be taken to a secure room and examined by medical personnel chosen by High Lord Greesh-Ka. They were sworn to secrecy and their findings delivered only to Skresh-Ka and High Lord Greesh-Ka. He watched as the three human captives were taken off the shuttle, carried on the shoulders of three strong Sook warriors. Skresh-Ka was undecided on the ultimate disposition of the captives. They had been used as shields, providing a means of escape for the members of the assault force. For now, they would be sent to a research facility and studied in the hopes that something could be discovered about the sudden appearance of the Anunnaki.

Startled by a muffled cough directly behind him, Skresh-Ka turned around and saw a tall Skarzi standing there. He was wearing a red sash across his chest, identifying him as a political envoy. Skresh-Ka hissed silently to himself, dreading what was to follow.

"Commander Skresh-Ka, I am Envoy Preesh and apologize for the intrusion. I am here to relay a message from the High Council. You are requested to appear before the Council at your earliest convenience", said Envoy Preesh, relaxing his stance as he waited for a reply.

"Thank you, Envoy Preesh. Inform the Council that I will appear before it after I've checked the status of the Assault team", replied Skresh-Ka, thinking it a good excuse. He needed more time to plan his defense.

"Thank you, Commander. I will relay your message to the Council. Welcome back", said Envoy Preesh, as he turned and left the hangar.

Skresh-Ka watched Envoy Preesh leave, a feeling of trepidation growing inside him. So it begins, he thought to himself as he began walking towards his office.

Chapter 24: Long Shot

Martin opened the door to his office and escorted Natasha into the conference room to await the arrival of the team. He noted that coffee and donuts were already laid out upon the table, Eva having done as asked.

"Thank you, Eva", said Martin, taking a seat at the head of the table and gesturing Natasha to take a seat next to him.

"You're welcome, Martin. The team should be arriving shortly", said Eva.

"I'm still not clear, as to what we can possibly do to help", said a puzzled Natasha.

"I too, have some doubts, but that's why I've called this meeting. The chance does exist that we can help and even if it's the remotest of chances, we owe it to the captives", replied Martin.

"I'll try to keep an open mind", replied Natasha with a smile.

Martin's heart lifted at the sight of Natasha's smile. He'd been having strange feelings lately, whenever he and Natasha were together. Feelings that he thought would never happen again. He'd also been thinking more often about his dead wife Susan, ever since the TimeBridge operation. He'd thought about her before, of course, but this seemed different. It was almost as if he'd lost her a few months ago, instead of the ten years that had already passed.

Martin smiled back at Natasha, just as Hiram Greenwood entered the room.

"Hello, Martin. Hello Natasha. Eva filled me in on what's been happening. I'm sorry to hear about General Esterbrook", said Hiram, as he took a seat across the table from Natasha.

"Hello, Hiram", said Natasha, her curiosity growing.

"Thank you for coming, Hiram. We're still waiting for Scott, Paul and Maggie. Feel free to have coffee and donuts", said Martin, noticing Hiram's slightly disheveled look.

Natasha shot Martin a questioning look at the mention of Maggie. Martin smiled back at Natasha, with eyes that hinted of hidden secrets.

Hiram plucked a doughnut from the tray and poured himself a cup of coffee adding cream and sugar. Scott entered the room moments later and took a seat next to Hiram.

"Hello, Scott. Thank you for coming. We are all sorry to hear about your father being captured", said a somber Martin.

"Hello, everyone and thank you. I'm not sure if there's anything we can do here", replied Scott, his voice heavy with sadness.

"Hang in there, Scott. Martin seems confident that we can do something", said Natasha, still not sure what Martin was planning.

"I'll do whatever it takes", said Scott as he poured himself a cup of coffee, black.

Paul and Maggie entered the room, taking seats across from Scott and Hiram.

"Hello everyone" said Paul and Maggie in unison. Everyone in the room returned the welcome as Maggie took the seat next to Natasha.

Paul gauged the atmosphere of the room, finding it a somber one, as he took a seat next to Maggie.

"Welcome, everyone. I'll start with the events that happened a few hours ago. Area 51 was attacked by an unknown alien race which disabled communications with the base and destroyed much of it. Casualties are around two hundred injured and sixty-three dead. General Esterbrook and two security officers were taken hostage, presumably after being used as human shields", said Martin.

"Human shields?" questioned Hiram.

"Yes. Apparently, the attackers were themselves attacked by an unknown force that destroyed some of the alien ships and many of the attacking aliens. General Esterbrook was used as cover for the attacking aliens to escape. I believe Paul can fill in a few of the blanks here", said Martin, looking at Paul.

Maggie squeezed Paul's hand under the table in a show of support.

Paul cleared his throat, quickly determining that this wasn't the time to come clean about his role in this. Secrecy would have to be maintained for now. He felt everyone's eyes on him as he readied a reply.

"From the reports that I've heard, it would seem that the attackers are Skarzi, as unbelievable as it sounds. It appears that they were here to retrieve the Skarzi body that was recovered after our Time-Bridge mission. The body must hold great value to the Skarzi, in order to launch such an attack. As to where they came from and most likely returned to, that would be Mars", said Paul. The reaction was initially disbelief, but soon changed to one of acceptance.

"Thank you, Paul. Hiram, I have a theoretical question. What would it take to generate a gateway to Mars?" asked Martin. He'd briefly entertained the idea of employing Project TimeBridge and just go back in time to change the current situation, but it just wasn't feasible and downright dangerous. The TimeBridge mission to ancient Jerusalem had proven that and was in fact, probably the cause of events at Area 51. No, there might be another way, which is what he was hoping Hiram would say.

Hiram paused and leaned forward, adjusted his glasses and thought about the question.

"Powering the gateway would take an immense amount of power, but with a sufficient number of QASM units, we should be able to do it. The Time-Bridge equipment should be able to supply ample power and is the best option. I can repurpose the current TimeBridge lab for this specific mission. The next thing would be the exact coordinates, since sub-surface Mars is basically unknown to us. I assume these Skarzi are underground, since we've never seen any sign of them on the surface. Environmentally, I would expect an Earth-like, tropical climate considering the reptilian nature of the Skarzi", replied Hiram, as he sat back in his chair.

"Thank you, Hiram. Scott, what would we need for a rescue team?" asked Martin.

"It would have to be a small team, between five and seven people. Any larger would risk discovery, endanger the mission and more importantly put the hostages at risk. Then, there are the obvious physical differences between us and the Skarzi. Being able to evade a passing glance would be a huge benefit to the operation", said Scott.

"Hmmmm. I think we can help with that. Dr. Morse has been able to merge meta-material technology into our DarkWeave suits. The result is a DarkWeave suit that renders the wearer invisible. To a passing gaze you wouldn't be there. It's also switchable, you can enable or disable the feature", replied Martin, receiving incredulous gazes from the team.

"Incredible!" answered Scott, hope showing in his eyes.

"I think we have a plan. The only thing missing are the coordinates. Paul, we need those coordinates. Contact Gabriel and see if he can help. Do whatever it takes to get them. Scott, see Dr. Morse about the suits. Ask for six. You, Paul and four members of the security team, then start getting the rescue team ready. Hiram, you can bring Time-Bridge out of mothball status and get us a gateway to Mars. That's all I have for now. Let's rescue the hostages!" said a confident Martin.

The team members filed out, each eager to fulfill their part of Martin's orders. Martin sensed a positive and hopeful attitude from them as they all filed out. He was happy that Paul had tailored his reply, refraining from mentioning anything about the

Antarctic cavern or possibly his involvement in the counter-attack. He had a suspicion that Paul had been involved, but other than confronting him outright, Martin wasn't sure what he could do. Then there was Natasha. Even though they had reached a level of amicability, Martin still harbored uncertainties about her allegiance to Majestic 12.

Martin's thoughts were interrupted by Natasha clearing her throat.

"I can see why you were hopeful. Your plan might just work. I have only one question. Who's Gabriel?" asked a curious Natasha.

Martin groaned inwardly. He'd assumed Natasha had been told about the Angels and how they had assisted DarkBridge Technology on occasion. He took a deep breath and launched into an explanation.

"It's like this....", said Martin as he began explaining. This was going to take some time, he thought to himself.

Chapter 25: Coordinates

Paul and Maggie left Martin's office, walking down the corridor, unsure as to their destination.

"We need the coordinates, but I'm not sure how to get in touch with Gabriel. He's always anticipated our needing him", said Paul.

"I'm sure Gabriel knows our intentions. How could he not, after spending so much time around us?" replied Maggie, as she reached out and squeezed Paul's hand.

They were both suddenly startled by someone clearing their throat behind them. So much so, that Maggie abruptly released Paul's hand. Turning around, they saw Gabriel standing behind them with a somber expression on his face.

"Gabriel!" exclaimed Paul.

"Hello Paul. Hello Maggie. I'm sorry to interrupt, but I sense that you need my assistance", said Gabriel. He and Raphael had discussed the possibility of a rescue attempt, both knowing that the humans might possibly attempt one. They were both in agreement that without some form of help, the rescue attempt would fail and the rescuers would most likely be killed. It would be easy for Gabriel or Raphael to kill the Skarzi and rescue the prisoners, but that would be a gross violation of the angel policy of non-interference. Gabriel wasn't about to kill any Skarzi and after talking with Raphael, it was agreed that they could offer some help by way of information. The information most useful to the humans would be the gateway coordinates that opened to the prisoner holding area. It was the best option to avoid casualties and keep within the policy of non-interference.

"Yes, we need your help Gabriel", said Maggie.

"Specifically, we need the coordinates where the prisoners are being held", said Paul.

"I can get those for you", replied Gabriel.

"Perfect. How soon can we have them?" asked an eager Paul.

"Give me a few minutes. I'll meet you in Maggie's apartment when I'm done", replied Gabriel.

"Thank you, Gabriel. This means a lot to us", said a serious Paul.

"You're welcome", replied Gabriel, pausing for a second, as he opened a gateway to Mars and stepped through.

"Hopefully, he can get us the coordinates", said Maggie.

"He'll come through. He always does", replied a confident Paul. Smiling, he grabbed Maggie's hand, the two of them walking back to her apartment to wait.

Gabriel exited the gateway and quickly closed it behind him. He found himself standing on the rocky soil of Mars, red dust billowing around him, as a small dust storm passed by. He felt the solar wind from the sun, bathing him in high energy electrons, akin to humans feeling a warm summer breeze. Basking in the free energy, he absorbed as much of it as possible. Energy was everything to beings like him and he took advantage of every opportunity to build and replenish his reserves.

He gazed around and spotted the edge of the canyon, where he and Raphael had spotted the Skarzi spacecraft leaving their underground hangar. Walking over to it, he stepped off the edge and floated down to where the massive hangar doors were. Putting his hand against the rocky facade, he sensed a large void on the opposite side, opened a gateway and stepped through. Exiting the gateway, he found himself inside a massive cavern, carved from solid rock. On the floor of the cavern sat spacecraft of all sizes, but there seemed to be a couple of empty berths. Probably belonging to the destroyed Skarzi spacecraft at Area 51, thought Gabriel to himself. There were thirty Skarzi warriors standing guard nearby, along with hundreds of Skarzi engineers performing various activities throughout the cavern. Gabriel was, of course, invisible and undetected by them. He floated into the air, altering his senses to detect the bio-signatures of the hostages. As he gazed around the cavern, his eyes located the transport ship that had been at Area 51. Three faint, human bio-signatures appeared near the ship, leading deeper into the cavern. Gabriel followed the faint trails, the deeper he traveled, the stronger the signals became.

The trails led to a large metal, reinforced door and Gabriel sensed activity coming from the other side. Concentrating, he opened a gateway, stepped through and exited on the other side of the door. He found himself in a wide tunnel, with six smaller tunnels that branched off from it. All the tunnels were well lit and he became conscious of the air itself. It would be breathable to humans, but humid. He hadn't given it much thought while he was in the hangar since he wasn't dependent on it for survival. This would be a plus for Paul and the rescue team.

One less thing to worry about, thought Gabriel. Numerous Skarzi could be seen entering and exiting the tunnels via side passageways. The trail was even stronger now and led down one of the six tunnels, branching off into a side passage. Gabriel traveled down the tunnel, following the trail into the side passage, which soon opened up into another large cavern. Large buildings lined a bustling thoroughfare, with hundreds of Skarzi walking along the thoroughfare, entering and exiting numerous buildings.

The scope of it all wasn't lost on Gabriel. The Skarzi had been busy over thousands of years, turning a small outpost into a teeming, thriving civilization. It worried Gabriel to think that at some point a schism may open between angels if the Skarzi pushed a war against the humans. All life was precious, a guiding tenant of the angels, but old wounds were slow to heal. The war between Annunaki and Skarzi so many thousands of years ago had left deep emotional wounds. Scores had died on both sides and for angels who were once Annunaki, those memories persisted. There would be angels embracing non-interference and on the other side, angels embracing action against the Skarzi. Sighing, Gabriel got back to the task at hand, locating the trail and following it to a large building with four burly Skarzi guards standing guard outside it.

Gabriel walked unseen, past the guards, entered the building and stood in what appeared to be a foyer.

Skarzi could be seen bustling about, some carrying various instruments, others carrying containers of what appeared to be food. Gabriel drifted up towards the ceiling, passing through it, to the floor above. Rising up, unseen through the floor, he found the end of the trail. Before him was a large, rectangular chamber, surrounded on all sides by a clear, glass-like barrier. Skarzi researchers were arranged around it, studying what lay on the other side. Gabriel walked over to the Skarzi researchers and stepped into a gap between them. Unseen by the Skarzi to his left and right, he could finally see the contents of the chamber.

What he saw confirmed his suspicions. The three human captives lay upon the floor, their bodies beginning to move, as they recovered from the effects of being stunned. Fortunately, the Skarzi hadn't begun any experiments yet, but that would soon change. Gabriel could only imagine what experiments the Skarzi would perform on the humans. Time would be critical, he thought to himself, as he noted the coordinates of the chamber. Mission complete, Gabriel opened a gateway back to Earth and Maggie's room, a pensive look on his face. Considerable danger would await the rescue team if they weren't careful. Stepping through the gateway, Gabriel vowed to make the rescue a success.

Chapter 26: Despair

General Esterbrook felt a cold sensation against the side of his face, a sign that his body was beginning to regain feeling. The fog of complete paralysis began to lift and consciousness slowly returned. As his mental fog cleared, he became more aware of his surroundings. He was lying sideways on some hard, cold surface, but the air around him felt warm and humid. Groaning sounds came from either side of him, a clear sign that his two security guards were coming around. His eyes slowly opened, unfocused at first, with only blurry images greeting his vision. He rolled onto his back and paused in discomfort, immediately becoming aware of multiple aches across his body. He felt like a sack of potatoes that had been tossed around. The weapons wielded by the aliens against them had been most effective, he thought to himself. A sharp pain from his right forearm intruded upon his thoughts. He raised his right forearm and rolled back the shirt sleeve. What he saw greatly concerned him.

There was a small surgical scar that had healed remarkably fast. Possibly some sort of implant, maybe a tracking device, he thought to himself. Glancing up, he saw white, sterile light shining down on him from some unknown lighting source. Pushing himself to a seating position, he began taking in his surroundings and as his vision cleared, his anxiety level also increased. He and his security guards were lying in some sort of chamber, maybe twenty feet by twenty feet, with clear walls on all four sides. At first, he could barely make out the dim shapes moving on the other side of the walls. Clarity returned to his vision, causing him to gasp at what he saw. Black, oval eyes stared at him from bodies that were clearly reptilian. Standing upright, the aliens were humanoid in appearance, but with green skin that seemed to be composed of very fine scales. They appeared similar to the alien creature transferred to Area 51 from DarkBridge Technology, which Paul had killed some three thousand years ago during the time of King Solomon.

Encountering strange creatures was part of the job at Area 51 and had given him a unique exposure to some strange alien creatures. Some had died as a result of their spacecraft crashing, others held captive for study. The alien creatures he was seeing now, represented a new race not recorded at Area 51. General Esterbrook had an idea though, as to who this alien species actually was. He'd read the reports Martin had sent him from DarkBridge Technology and knew these aliens to be called "Skarzi". They were obviously behind the attack on Area 51 and were now his captors. As he looked through the clear wall in front of him, a group of five Skarzi approached and stood on the other side of the clear wall observing the three captives. One of the five Skarzi appeared to be someone of rank, with medals adorning the uniform it wore. The others, he could only speculate as to whom they were, but odds put them as some sort of researchers.

Motion on his left and right caught his attention, as the two security guards maneuvered to a sitting position.

"I feel as if someone hit my head with a sledgehammer", groaned the guard to his right.

"Not a sledgehammer, but a Mack truck", echoed the guard on his left, as he held his head.

"Are you okay, General?" asked the guard on his left.

"Yes, I'm okay, just recovering from the same headache. I have some bad news though. It appears that we are being held captive by a race of alien creatures. The same ones that attacked Area 51", said General Esterbrook.

Both security guards inhaled deeply, as they glanced around their glass prison.

"Can we escape?" asked the security guard to his right.

"We could try, but we wouldn't get very far. We don't know where we are, or if we are still on Earth. We could be on some strange planet for all we know", said the General.

No sooner had the General spoken, when a portion of the glass wall slid away and six burly aliens strode in brandishing large evil-looking weapons. Two of the aliens walked over to the security guard on his left, hauled him to his feet and began dragging him away. The security guard yelled and struggled valiantly, but it was of little avail against the overwhelming strength of the aliens. The other four aliens took positions in front of General Esterbrook and the remaining security guard, ending any thought of saving the other guard.

General Esterbrook watched as the security guard was hauled through the opening in the wall and taken down a long corridor, still struggling to get free. He lost sight of the security guard just as the four aliens guarding them retreated, closing the opening in the wall behind them. General Ester-brook felt despair and fear growing inside him, as he realized that they may have become experimental lab rats. He resigned himself to the fact that no one would be coming to save them. Their nightmare had just begun.

Chapter 27: Black and White

Black, the entity from the dark matter universe, sped through the vast expanse of space, heading towards a solar system in an outer arm of the Milky Way galaxy. In human terms, Black had left that same solar system many thousands of years ago. Having released itself from a containment vessel and finding little of technological value on Earth, it had traveled to Mars. There, it found sentient beings called the Skarzi, capable of interplanetary travel. Black had high hopes, but those hopes were soon dashed soon after arrival. It had found the Skarzi, living beneath the surface and still clinging to ancient, rigid social classifications. Their level of technology had allowed them to build a working, thriving society beneath the Martian surface. Even here on Mars, Black still wasn't impressed, finding the level of technology rather unsatisfying and well below the level that would satisfy its reconnaissance mission goals.

Disappointed, Black had left the planet Mars, and headed into deep space, on a search for the origins of the Annunaki and Skarzi races. Curiosity drove it and Black had plenty of time, which held no meaning for an entity of the dark matter universe. After crossing the vastness of space, Black had arrived at the Annunaki home world of Innunak and found it relatively devoid of life, with large craters dotting the surface and any structures reduced to rubble. Apparently, the Annunaki had been destroyed in some massive attack, but Black was curious as to why there wasn't some small remnant of Annunaki civilization left. It was as if the Annunaki had disappeared before the destruction. Disappointed, Black left the planet and sought out the Skarzi home world next.

Arriving at the Skarzi planet, Black once again observed a devastated surface, devoid of life. Large swaths of the surface had been blown away, by some powerful weapon, and any structures also reduced to rubble. To Black, it appeared that both civilizations had destroyed one another in some final cataclysmic battle. Black had hovered above the Skarzi home world, unsure as to what to do next. It had traveled all this way only to be met with disappointment, irking Black to no end. So it had drifted among the stars in search of a new direction. Finding none, Black made the decision to return to the same solar system it had left. In human terms, the intervening time since it had left would equate to some three thousand years, by the time it arrived there. Black thought that enough time to see some technological advances from the Skarzi and maybe even the humans. With renewed curiosity, Black began the journey back.

The space where Black had just occupied began to ripple, coalescing into a beautiful woman, clothed in a gleaming white gown sprinkled with stars and long black hair that spilled about her shoulders. Celestra watched as Black departed, her thoughts shifting to the planets that Black had visited. While not uncommon for civilizations to rise and fall, it still saddened Celestra to see it occur because of war between species. Both the Annunaki and Skarzi civilizations had evolved in the same constellation, but in different star systems. That the two would eventually war with one another was inevitable. Intelligence didn't always translate to peaceful coexistence and somewhere back in their histories, the two had initially met. That meeting had probably set each civilization on a path towards finding out who was the superior race.

After much war, the Annunaki had eventually ascended to a higher state of existence, where it was hoped that they would find enlightenment. The Skarzi hadn't been as fortunate, their physical bodies destroyed, their souls had been sent to a new planet. There, they would be reborn and begin existence as a new species and hopefully not repeating their prior mistakes. It was as it had always been since her father had created the universe, the cycle of life, death and rebirth. Sighing, she shifted her gaze back towards the departing Black, the dark matter entity. Another of her father's creations, dark matter was as important to the universe as all the other myriad of particles comprising it. That a form of intelligent life had risen from it was a source of great pride with her father, the Creator. The same cycle driving life also drove the universe, except on a significantly grander scale, she thought to herself.

Watching from a distance, it was obvious that Black was headed towards a distant solar system, one that was located in the same spiral arm of the galaxy and one that Celestra had many reasons to visit. One reason, which she wasn't exactly sure why, was to look in on the Annunaki pilot she had rescued from certain death. Maybe it was curiosity, but she thought it might be something more, something she wasn't quite ready to acknowledge. The other reason was family related. Her brother had been causing much trouble even in captive exile and needed a tighter leash. Looking at the Annunaki and Skarzi civilizations, she could see the hand of her brother involved in the conflict. Lucifer will be surprised to see her, she thought to herself with a smile. The space around her began to ripple once again, her form faded away as she followed Black towards the distant solar system.

Chapter 28: Rescue Prelude

Paul and Maggie reached her apartment, both feeling a tension between them. Entering, they took a seat, sitting side by side on the living room sofa. Paul looked at Maggie, noting her pensive expression. Captivated by her beauty and long blonde hair spilling about her shoulders, he somehow found the willpower to put a voice to that tension.

"I know you'd like to go on this mission, Maggie, but it's just too dangerous for both of us to go. We need you here in case we need to wake Commander Kalon and ask for his help. He'd be more likely to help if you were the one to ask", said Paul.

"I know you're right, but I want to feel like more of a contributor here. I just don't feel like I contribute much", replied Maggie.

"Don't ever think that. You're an important member of the team and could hold the key to the survival of our planet", said Paul, as he brushed her hair away and kissed her. Maggie responded with a hug and a kiss of her own, just as the room was enveloped in a golden glow and a gateway appeared in a corner of the room.

Gabriel stepped out of the gateway, saw the two of them sitting on the sofa and immediately sensed some important discussion had taken place. If this wasn't of extreme importance, he might've quickly stepped back through the gateway and left them in peace. Unfortunately, the extreme importance of his visit required the interruption.

"Hello Paul. Hello Maggie. I've found what you need", said Gabriel, as he assembled the coordinates mentally.

"That's fantastic! This was the only thing holding us back", said an excited Paul.

"Are the General and his security guards okay?" asked a genuinely concerned Maggie.

"Yes, the General and the two security guards are okay. They are still recovering from the effects of the Skarzi stun weapons, but are still in great danger. They are being held in a Skarzi research building that appears to specialize in biological experiments. Given their location, I estimate it only a matter of time before the experiments begin. One of the security guards appears to have been through some sort of examination already and seems to be drugged", replied Gabriel.

Paul and Maggie's faces went ashen at the thought of biological experiments being conducted on the abductees.

"We have to move now", said Paul with a sense of urgency, as Maggie gripped his hand in a show of support.

"I agree. I will place the coordinates in Eva's quantum memory storage, where she will find it readily accessible. Normally, I would give them to you directly, but due to their complexity, any error could prove disastrous", said Gabriel.

"Thank you, Gabriel. I'll alert Martin and the rest of the team", replied Paul.

"Excellent. Give me a few seconds to place the coordinates", replied Gabriel, as he turned and stepped through the gateway, closing it behind him.

A golden glow enveloped the computer room, as Gabriel stepped out of the gateway. Glancing around, Gabriel located Eva's quantum processors and memory storage. Pausing, he took a moment to assess recent strides in human technology. While primitive compared to Annunaki technology, he still found it rather impressive. Locating the quantum memory storage unit, Gabriel touched it, sensing the complex circuitry inside. He concentrated, sending his mind deep into Eva's quantum memory, looking for a place to store the coordinates. He found an area of memory related to Mars and placed the coordinates there, flagging it as high importance. The keyword would be Mars and when mentioned, it would unlock the coordinates in her memory. Satisfied, Gabriel withdrew his mind and returned to Maggie's apartment.

Paul and Maggie were still sitting on the sofa processing what Gabriel had said, when a golden glow once again filled the room. Gabriel stepped out and smiled.

"The coordinates have been placed in Eva's memory. The trigger word is "Mars" and upon hearing it, the coordinates will unlock", said Gabriel.

"Thank you, Gabriel. Will you be following Paul to Mars?" asked Maggie.

"Yes, but I'm limited in what I can do. For instance, I cannot take a Skarzi life", said Gabriel.

"At least you'll be there to offer some form of assistance", replied Maggie, her shoulders slumping as some tension left her.

"Yes, I will keep an eye on him", answered Gabriel, expressing what Maggie really wanted to hear.

"Thank you, Gabriel. I'll start getting ready", said Paul, as he rose from the sofa.

"Yes, thank you Gabriel", said a relieved Maggie.

"I'll be waiting for you in the lab on Mars, while keeping an eye on the abductees. Good luck, and I'll see you there", said Gabriel with a wave, as he stepped through the gateway and closed it behind him.

Paul watched Gabriel leave, a mix of anticipation, excitement and trepidation settling over him.

Maggie walked over to the closet and pulled out Paul's camouflage outfit, along with the latest version of DarkWeave suit and handed both to him.

He quickly changed out of his current Dark-Weave suit and into this latest version. He then put his camouflage outfit on and pressed a button on the DarkWeave collar, but nothing seemed to happen.

Maggie however, saw something different.

"Paul? Where are you! Are you still here?" asked a concerned Maggie. One moment Paul was here and the next he was gone.

"Yes, I'm still here. Dr. Morse has really created something remarkable here, with these new Dark-Weave suits, came Paul's disembodied voice. He was doubly impressed with the new suit. The stealth mode field extended beyond the the Dark-Weave suit to encompass whatever exterior clothing was being worn. The effect was complete invisibility. Amazing, thought Paul.

"I can't see you at all!" replied a surprised Maggie.

"Here I am", said Paul, as he turned off the suit's stealth mode.

"Thank you, sweetheart. It was getting a little unnerving, hearing a voice and not seeing a body to go with it", replied Maggie, relieved at Paul's reappearance.

"Back to the business at hand. Eva, do you have the Mars coordinates?" asked Paul.

"Hello, Paul. Coordinates? What coordinates are you referring to? Wait. What's this? I don't remember placing any coordinates for Mars in my memory. Yet here they are. Yes, I have them. Gateway coordinates to someplace under the surface of Mars. It's very strange that I don't remember. I'll have to run some internal diagnostics", replied Eva with some puzzlement.

"Don't worry too much about it Eva. Stranger things have happened", said Paul, holding back about Gabriel's intrusion into her memory. After the intrusion by Asmodeus during the TimeBridge incident, Paul wasn't sure how Eva would take another such intrusion.

"Thank you, Paul. I'm projecting a 75 percent chance that you and the team are going to have a successful rescue on Mars. There's still a 25 percent chance of failure", said Eva.

"You'll have to work on your optimism Eva. 75 percent is still pretty good. Contact Martin, Scott and Hiram. Tell them you have the coordinates.

Maggie and I are headed to the TimeBridge lab", said Paul, as he and Maggie left her apartment.

"All set, Paul. Good luck!" replied Eva.

"Thank you, Eva. We'll need it", replied Paul. He remembered the last mission using the TimeBridge portal and how he had come close to dying. Hopefully, this time would be different, thought Paul as they headed towards the lab.

Chapter 29: Dark Thoughts

Skresh-Ka stood in front of the reinforced, glass containment room, watching the humans. Flanked by Skarzi researchers and his bodyguards, they watched as the humans slowly recovered from the effects of the stun weapons. Adorned in medals, Skresh-Ka was a striking figure, standing out from those around him. Skresh-Ka noticed one of the humans give him an appraising glance. Obviously, it was a human that knew authority when it saw it. It could even be that this human was of some importance. Skresh-Ka scoffed at the thought, silently laughing to himself at the absurdity of a human holding importance as great as his own.

His thoughts drifted to his ancestor, Captain Skresh and how the humans had somehow come across his remains. It could be that one or more of the three humans had some part in the study of those remains. Earlier, Skresh-Ka had visited one of the other research labs where those remains had been taken. Skresh-Ka had seen the gleaming, white cylinder sitting on a low table and had walked over to it. Peering inside, through a glass window set into the cylinder, Skresh-Ka saw the remains of his ancestor. After three thousand human years, the body was still recognizable, albeit somewhat des-iccated. He ran a scaled claw, reverently along the metallic surface, anger growing inside him, as he saw the surgical cuts made into the body. The humans had sliced through the now in-operable, self-heal-ing body armor. Barbarians! Desecrators! No respect for the dead, thought Skresh-Ka. Anger growing in-side him, he had turned away from the cylinder and left the lab, quickly making his way to the research room containing the human captives. Death was on his mind.

Skresh-Ka ordered the room cleared, his anger growing, violent thoughts filling his mind. He was about to pull out his energy weapon and vaporize the humans, when something unexpected hap-pened. Someone cleared their throat behind him with a hiss, jolting Skresh-Ka from his dark thoughts, causing him to turn around. It was that blasted emissary, Envoy Preesh, from the High Council.

"Excuse me, Commander. The High Council is demanding your appearance", said the emissary.

"The Council can wait. This is important", replied Skresh-Ka.

"I'm sorry Commander but you don't understand. It's not a request. It's an order", replied the emissary.

Skresh-Ka let out a deep hiss. His desire to exterminate the humans would have to wait.

"All right, let's go", said an angry Skresh-Ka, as he stormed out of the lab, followed at a short distance by the emissary.

Skresh-Ka put some distance between him and the emissary, exiting the building and quickly reaching his ground car. Climbing in, medals jiggling, he closed the door, giving instructions to his driver. The ground car zipped away, just as the emissary reached it, leaving him behind, red Martian dust swirling around him. The emissary coughed, searching around for another ground car to no avail. Frustrated, the emissary could only watch, as the Commander's ground car sped away. Skresh-Ka sat in the ground car deep in thought, as it sped through the cavern towards his meeting with the High Council. That he was ordered to appear before the High Council didn't sound good. It was usually sent as a request, not an order. This sounded ominous and most likely it was related to the assault mission. High Lord Greesh-Ka probably had something to do with it, thought Skresh-Ka as he contemplated his defense.

Chapter 30:
Redemption

The car sped through the Sath science cavern, passed through a long connecting tunnel and emerged into the Skom political cavern. Skresh-Ka had decided on ground transportation instead of the more public transport module in order to reduce any public appearances and forgo any embarassment. The Council summons had sounded grave and many in the Skom cavern might aleady be aware of it. The ground car soon reached its destination, stopping in front of the High Council building. Skresh-Ka exited the ground car, pausing to straighten out his uniform and medals.

Projecting an air of confidence and putting some swagger into his step, he entered the building and made his way to the High Council chamber. Skresh-Ka reached the chamber, its tall, metal doors closed and guarded by two council guards on either side. Seeing Skresh-Ka approach, the two guards saluted, grabbed the door handles and swung the heavy metal doors open. Skresh-Ka returned the salute and strode through the doors, into the Council chambers. Once again, he found himself standing before the High Council.

Skresh-Ka surveyed the seated council members, arranged in a semi-circle before him. High Lord Greesh-Ka sat in the middle, directly in front of him, a withering stare emanating from him. Skresh-Ka was beginning to buckle under that stare, but found some inner bluster.

"High Lords, why have I been summoned before you?" asked Skresh-Ka, trying to project some authority.

High Lord Greesh-Ka leaned back in his chair, his green, scaled claws clenching and unclenching with barely contained anger.

"Commander Skresh-Ka. You've been summoned before the Council to answer for your actions and the debacle that took place on Earth", boomed the voice of High Lord Greesh-Ka.

"Debacle? I successfully retrieved the artifact and leveled the human installation. I consider it an unqualified success", said Skresh-Ka.

"At what cost? Ships lost, warriors lost and evidence of Annunaki technology being used against you. Not to mention how you fled from the planet when presented with the mere appearance of an overwhelming threat. I would call it an unmitigated disaster", replied an angry Greesh-Ka.

"I was as surprised as anyone when the Anunnaki craft showed up and destroyed most of my surface ships. Then, I felt there wasn't any other choice but to flee, when over 200 hundred fighters started coming towards the Ketska. The ship was in serious danger of being destroyed", replied a defensive Skresh-Ka.

High Lord Greesh-Ka stared at Commander Skresh-Ka, his reptilian eyes narrowing to slits in disgust.

"Commander, we've reviewed all the sensor data from the Ketska, including our own observations from our monitoring satellites. It is our belief that there were only five real Anunnaki spacecraft involved and all the rest were diversionary drones. Five real fighters is hardly an overwhelming force. Surely, the Ketska with its mighty firepower could have dealt with only five fighters, don't you agree? Additionally, in referencing the ancient archives regarding the war with the Annunaki, we came across instances of similar drone usage. It had been used quite effectively against us numerous times. Quite a few of those times were used by one Annunaki pilot called Captain Valinor. Of course, he is long dead, but it is troubling that such tactics were used against us once again" said High Lord Greesh-Ka, as he watched Skresh-Ka squirm with fear.

Skresh-Ka was shaken by the news and barely able to stand. Only five fighters? All the rest just a simple diversionary tactic? The same tactics used in ancient times by someone named Valinor? Skresh-Ka felt his military command and accomplishments slipping away as he thought about the consequences. What the High Lord implied was tantamount to cowardice in the face of battle. His reason for fleeing had been based on the overwhelming odds the Ketska would face.

"High Lords, I did what I thought best for the Ketska and the mission", replied Skresh-Ka in defense.

Reptilian hisses of disgust erupted from the other High Council Lords. High Lord Greesh-Ka raised his green scaled hand, bringing the other High Lords to silence.

"Commander, it is our belief that you should no longer....", High Lord Greesh-Ka's voice trailed off as he cocked his head to one side, listening to his communication implant. His reptilian eyes opened wide with shock and he let out a sharp hiss.

Straightening his head, he regarded Skresh-Ka, formulating new plans for the Commander.

"High Lords, there has been an incident at the biological lab containing the human captives. Evidently, the humans have other Annunaki technology, as well as their spacecraft. The human prisoners have been freed and are no longer on this planet. They were freed by elements from their own planet, by means we are not quite sure of yet", said High Lord Greesh-Ka, pausing to let the information sink in.

The other High Lords leaned back in their chairs, reptilian eyes wide with shock.

Skresh-Ka felt anger rising within him. Had he been left with the humans a bit longer, they would be dead, denying the rescuers any satisfaction.

"Commander, in light of this new information and obvious threat to our security, we have no choice, but to get the fleet ready for attack. Since you are still the senior commander, I order you to the asteroid belt. Prepare the fleet for war. Make whatever preparations you need to get the fleet ready. Consider this a reprieve and a chance at redemption.

Skresh-Ka couldn't believe it. One minute everything was falling apart for him and now he had been given a chance to regain everything and become a hero. His ancestor, Captain Skresh must be looking out for him.

"Thank you, council members. I won't let you down", replied a confident Skresh-Ka.

"See that you don't Commander. The consequences will be even more dire for you, should you fail", said High Lord Greesh-Ka.

Skresh-Ka bowed, turned and left the Council chambers, his thoughts turning to the fleet and the work that still remained.

Reaching his ground car, he climbed in and settled into the plush cushions. His thoughts briefly turned towards the lab and how the humans had managed a rescue. It was troubling to say the least and hinted at some unknown technology in the hands of a decidedly inferior race. A lizard-like smile formed on his face as his thoughts turned back to the council chamber. He would have the last laugh on High Lord Greesh-Ka. It would be Commander Skresh-Ka, hero to the Skarzi! Long live Commander Skresh-Ka! He signaled to his driver and the ground car zipped away, the High Council building growing smaller and smaller, as they headed back to Sook territory.

The gound car reached the large underground hangar in the Sook cavern, stopping near the command shuttle to drop off Skresh-Ka before driving away. Skresh-Ka stood before his command shuttle, pondering whether he should remain here before departing for the asteroid belt. There really wasn't much choice, he thought to himself. There was much to do in order to get the fleet ready and time wasn't on his side. High Lord Greesh-Ka and the other council members were looking for any reason to demote him and procrastination would be at the top of the list. No, best to get moving and get the fleet in shape, thought Skresh-Ka.

He walked up the ramp and boarded the shuttle, taking a seat in one of the plusher seats near a view port. The pilot, already on board, closed the entry door, retracted the boarding ramp and fired up the shuttle's manuevering engines. The shuttle lifted gently off the ground, floating towards the large hangar doors that were already sliding open. Skresh-Ka watched from the view port, as the shuttle passed through the massive doors, always awed by the magnificence of Skarzi technology. Once free of the hangar doors, the shuttle pilot engaged the main engines and began a rapid ascent into the upper atmosphere.

Skresh-Ka looked out the view port, watching the planet Mars recede behind the shuttle and the distance between him and his beloved Sareesh growing by the second. There hadn't been time to say goodbye, but maybe he could send a message from the KetSka when he arrived. Soon the blackness of space engulfed the shuttle and Skresh-Ka's mood began to change. He'd left the High Council chamber in a mood bordering on ebullient, but that mood was beginning to sour and even his plush seat offered little comfort. The more he thought about it, the more he thought it a fool's task and a recipe for disaster. The fleet still wasn't ready for such a massive undertaking, with problems ranging from staffing shortages to battle cruisers still under construction. Skresh-Ka watched the stars passing by, his thoughts growing more pessimistic the closer the shuttle got to the asteroid belt. Yes, the Skarzi were on the way, but in what capacity, thought Skresh-Ka, as he settled into his plush chair and tried to take a nap.

Chapter 31: The Portal

Martin stood in the TimeBridge lab, waiting patiently for Paul to arrive, which would complete the rescue team. Recently mothballed due to recent events, the lab had been reactivated for this special mission. Natasha stood next to him, close enough, that he found the scent of her perfume almost intoxicating. They had become close, but the capture of Bob Esterbrook had put any thoughts of romance on hold for the time being. Martin looked over at Scott Esterbrook, the head of DarkBridge security. Scott seemed to be maintaining a detached, professional facade, but Martin could see the strain etched on his face. He could only imagine the toll this was of having on Scott. To have ones father captured and possibly experimented on made Martin shiver. He looked around the lab and saw Hiram sitting in front of a bank of virtual displays, monitoring the charge levels of the multiple QASM units attached to the TimeBridge portal. Martin briefly thought about renaming it, possibly to MarsBridge, but somehow it didn't quite have the same ring to it.

Moments later, Paul and Maggie entered the room. Paul was dressed for combat, while Maggie was wearing casual clothing. That was a relief, thought Martin. Paul must have convinced her to stay behind. Otherwise, it may have fallen on Martin to make the call. It was bad enough that he might lose six people on a highly dangerous rescue mission. To also lose Maggie, would be an unimaginable loss to those who knew her, not to mention her father, Thomas Stanton who would hold Martin fully accountable.

The team was complete and it was time to go. Scott passed an assault rifle and rucksack to Paul containing extra diamene coated ammo clips and a few other assorted items. Martin noted that the entire team was wearing the newest version of DarkWeave suits. Dr. Morse, head of the Applied Materials Division, wasn't giving any guarantees on protection from energy weapons. There had been survivors in the defense of Area 51 and all had been wearing DarkWeave suits. That had sounded promising for the rescue team, but Dr. Morse still had reservations about close proximity energy discharges. Maybe the new DarkWeave stealth technology would offset that. Martin wasn't sure, but there was only one way to find out.

"How do we look, Hiram?" asked Martin, has he turned towards his good friend.

"All QASM units fully charged and ready!" replied Hiram in an overly excited voice. He'd managed to convert most of the TimeBridge equipment over to the Mars mission and was fairly satisfied in its operation. There would never be 100 percent certainty, but it was as close as he could get, given the brief time frame.

Martin looked at Scott, who gave him the "thumbs up" sign, signaling that the team was ready.

"Good luck, everyone. We don't know what dangers you'll face on Mars, but safety first. This is a hostage rescue. If things get too rough, save the team, leave the hostages. We'll figure out another rescue attempt. Remember, the portal will open again in thirty minutes. Be ready for transfer back here. Try not to miss it. We don't know when we'll be able to reopen it", said Martin, gauging the reactions from the team.

"We'll do our best, Martin", said Scott, unsure if he could really leave his father behind.

"Thank you, Scott. Our thoughts and prayers go with you and the team", replied Martin.

"Ready, Martin", said Hiram, as he adjusted his eyeglasses.

"Okay. Open the portal", said Martin.

Hiram pressed a couple of keys on one of the virtual displays, which began sending increasing levels of modulated power to the TimeBridge archway. A purplish glow began to surround the archway and a light blue shimmer began forming inside the archway. Power levels increased to the archway, causing the light bluish shimmer to darken.

The archway rippled and an energy pulse shot through the lab, raising the hair on Martin's and others arms. The archway turned to dark blue color, signaling stabilization.

"Archway stabilized. Ready for transfer!" said an excited Hiram.

Scott signaled the team forward, taking point and being the first to enter the portal.

Each team member followed, with Paul bringing up the rear. Paul turned to Maggie and smiled, with Maggie smiling back. He stepped through the portal as it quickly closed behind him.

"Godspeed", said Martin, as he and the others found a place to sit while waiting for the team to return.

Hiram began recharging the QASM modules, preparing for the next portal opening and hopefully the return of the team.

"I hope they're successful", said Natasha as she pulled up a chair next to Martin.

"They will succeed. Gabriel will be there to help", said Maggie, as she too pulled up a chair alongside Martin.

Martin hoped that Maggie was correct, as he settled back in his chair. These next thirty minutes were going to seem like an eternity.

Chapter 32:
Rescue

Scott Esterbrook, head of security at DarkBridge Technology, was the first to exit the gateway. His military training took over and he immediately dropped to a crouching position, scanning the area for threats. The rest of the team followed, mimicking his crouching stance. Scott surveyed the area, which appeared to be some sort of lab. Rows of metallic benches were lined up facing what appeared to be some sort of glass enclosed confinement room. He could see his father and the two security guards lying on the floor of the confinement room, a round metal container set against a far wall, possibly used for urination needs. Scott let out a sigh of relief, as he saw that they were still alive, but anger grew inside him at the inhumane treatment of the captives. They lacked any kind of bedding, lying prone on the hard floor and no liquid or food nourishment visible. Evidently, their captors considered them to be little more than animals.

Paul, the last of the team members to exit the now closed gateway, tapped Scott on the shoulder, pointing to a couple of reptilian, Skarzi guards lounging near a far entrance to the lab. They appeared confident that a prisoner escape was impossible, along with any type of rescue attempt. They also seemed to be oblivious to the gateway that had just opened, disgorging the rescue team. Scott nodded and signaled for two of the other team members to eliminate the Skarzi guards. The two team members fanned out and enabled stealth mode on their DarkWeave suits. Unseen to the Skarzi, each member targeted one of the guards with their assault rifles, which were loaded with diamene ammo. One shot from each team member caught the Skarzi guards by surprise, diamene bullets slicing cleanly through the Skarzi body armor, passing right through their hearts. At first the Skarzi seemed unaffected, so clean was the bullet entry, but soon the guards began jerking around and randomly firing their energy weapons into the air. Energy discharges turned areas of the metal ceiling into molten slag, as the guards suddenly fell to the ground dead, succumbing to their wounds. Fortunately the energy discharges were brief, otherwise the ceiling might have caved in. The two team members, made their way silently back to the group, turned off stealth mode and awaited further commands.

Paul was amazed at the lack of Skarzi in the lab. Other than the two Skarzi guards, the lab was deserted. Obviously, the Skarzi had considered a rescue attempt far beyond any human capability. He was also fascinated with how the team members had just disappeared when stealth mode was enabled. It was one thing to be inside the suit when it was enabled, but a whole different experience when viewed as an onlooker. Most effective. Paul looked around the lab, searching for Gabriel and spotted him standing in a far corner, observing the situation. He wasn't sure if Gabriel would intercede if things went south, but it didn't seem to be an issue right now. Anything could happen, as he knew all too well.

Scott stood up and the rest of the team followed suit, as he walked towards the glass enclosure. Standing before the glass enclosure, he began pounding on the glass, trying to awaken the captives. He saw his father, Bob Esterbrook, begin to stir, along with his two security guards. Scott took the butt of his assault rifle and brought it heavily against the glass wall. Nothing happened, except for a dull ring from the glass. Scott stood back, impressed with the strength of the glass. His father was now sitting up, along with the two security guards, clearly confused as to what was happening.

"We'll have to melt our way through", said Paul in a low, quiet voice.

"Yes. Give me your backpack", replied Scott in an equally quiet voice, as he pulled on a pair of Dark-Weave gloves.

Paul complied, removing the backpack from his shoulders. Scott pulled out a coiled, gray, corded substance from the backpack and began unwinding it. He motioned Paul to hold the remaining cord, as he took one end and pressed it against the bottom of the glass. Scott continued pressing the cord against the glass, drawing it from the dwindling coil in Paul's hands. Scott finished pressing the cord against the glass and stood back. He had formed the outline of a doorway and was now ready to ignite the thermal cord. Rooting around in Paul's backpack once again, Scott found the thermal igniter and remote control. Paul watched as Scott pressed the thermal igniter into the cord at the bottom of the glass and then signaled everyone to stand back. He then motioned the three men in the chamber to get back against the far wall.

The three men in the chamber seemed rejuvenated at the thought of freedom and quickly moved to the far wall, crouching and covering their heads.

Scott pressed a button on the remote, triggering the thermal igniter, which lit up the length of the cord in a blinding white light. Burning at over three thousand degrees Celsius, the thermal cord melted through the glass wall, forming a ragged doorway. Scott quickly moved forward, catching the melted section of glass with his DarkWeave gloves, before it fell and caused someone to investigate the sound. Silence was still critical and Scott couldn't risk being discovered at such a critical moment.

Bob Esterbrook had been resting on the hard floor, feelings of depression setting in as he considered their impossible predicament. Fortunately, the security guard had been returned to the prison alive, except for some bruises and a drugged look. There was no way he could allow this to continue, either by experimentation or worse, dissection. That thought alone made his empty stomach turn. He wasn't sure how he could prevent any of it from happening, except for maybe murder/suicide. Since they didn't have weapons, someone would have to strangle two of the hostages and then commit suicide. It was a bleak, grisly prospect and probably impossible to complete, given the circumstances. He'd almost given up all hope, when a brief flash caught his eye. He sat up, noticing camouflage figures exiting a gateway, fanning out and dropping to crouching positions.

His eyes wandered to a far door where two of the reptilian Skarzi guards were stationed and who seemed to be discussing something between them, oblivious to what was taking place. He saw two of the camouflaged figures move closer and then miraculously disappear. Then he saw two muzzle flashes and the two Skarzi dropped dead to the ground, but not until haphazardly firing their energy weapons. The two camouflaged figures reappeared and rejoined the group. One of the camouflaged figures came up to the glass confinement chamber and began banging it with the butt of his rifle. It took a few moments before Bob recognized the figure as his son Scott. A tear ran down his face, as he realized that Scott had come to rescue him.

Scott, still holding the large glass cutout with his DarkWeave gloves, sighed with relief, as Paul came up from behind, also wearing DarkWeave gloves and helped him. The two of them moved the heavy, glass pane and leaned it against an adjacent glass wall. The security guard prisoners rose and helped the General to his feat, all three unsteadily walking over to their doorway to freedom. Scott stood there, as each security guard shook his hand in gratitude for freeing them from a fate worse than death. Last in line was Scott's father with emotion clearly etched on his face.

"Hi, Dad", said Scott, barely controlling his emotions.

"Hello, son", replied Bob Esterbrook, as he engulfed Scott in a big hug of thanks.

Scott held his dad for a few moments, but pulled away as the reality of their situation intruded.

"We have five minutes before the gateway reopens. We need to be close to where it first opened, but not too close", said Scott loud enough so that everyone could hear. It was hard to believe that so much time had already passed, thought Scott to himself.

The prisoners moved out of the confinement chamber, assisted by Scott and Paul to a position close to the awaited gateway. The other rescue team members took up guard positions around the group in case of a Skarzi attack. Minutes later and right on time, a familiar shimmering blue gateway formed and stabilized. Scott led his father and the security guards through first, followed by the rescue team.

Paul was the last to enter the gateway, buoyed by the success of the mission. He glanced at his friend Gabriel before entering the gateway, but saw him obscured by some dark cloud-like mass. As Paul watched, Gabriel seemed to be struggling against the cloud-like mass. Alarmed, Paul was ready to try and intercede, but Gabriel waved him away, motioning for him to go. Paul, torn between helping his friend or returning to Maggie and completing the mission, reluctantly stepped through the gateway. His friend Gabriel was on his own.

Chapter 33:
Attacked

Black entered the solar system, pausing at what the humans called the rings of Jupiter. Familiarity came to Black, as it surveyed the area. Further in, tucked within the asteroid belt, Black detected the energy patterns coming from multiple Skarzi battle cruisers. It seemed that the civilization it had once visited so long ago, had survived and grown. Black's attention quickly shifted to the fourth planet called Mars, as a brief, powerful energy surge came and abruptly disappeared. Black had once visited the same planet long ago in order to assess its technology level, but this energy was different, more powerful. It was unlike anything previously exhibited by the reptilian Skarzi and seemed beyond their level of technology. That was, unless of course, the Skarzi had made some significant technological advances since then. Intrigued, Black sped towards the anomalous energy surge on the fourth planet, eager to see what had caused it.

Celestra, shadowing Black, watched as the dark matter being paused, then sped towards the fourth planet in this solar system. She too had detected the energy surge, but unlike Black, knew much more about what was going on in this solar system. Black was trouble though, a clear threat to anything and everyone in this solar system, not to mention the entire universe. There was no choice but to follow and repair whatever damage Black would cause. At the moment their paths were intertwined and eventually she would have to take more drastic action, but not just yet.

Black reached Mars and descended to the surface, pausing to sense the energy levels below the surface. Black knew the Skarzi were there, but there was something else there as well, something with a large store of energy, something somewhat familiar. Black, almost depleted of energy after its interstellar travel, began phasing with the Mars surface, descending through the sandy, red soil to the world below. Black eventually passed through a cavern ceiling, paused, then floated towards a Skarzi building. The energy source was indeed familiar, similar to the one he had once fed on called Lilith. This energy source seemed slightly different and stronger, which only increased Black's hunger. Black passed through the thick metal walls of the building and found the source of the energy.

Gabriel watched as the rescue team exited the gateway and he quickly weaved an aura of disinterest around the two Skarzi guards. The two guards, completely disinterested in their surroundings, were soon dispatched by two of the human team members. Those same two members of the rescue team had disappeared from normal view during the killing and then had suddenly reappeared. Obviously, the humans had enhanced their DarkWeave suits to include visual cloaking. Impressed with their technology, speed and efficiency, Gabriel continued watching as the one called Scott freed his father and the two security guards. It looked like the rescue team had taken advantage of the Skarzi disinterest and eliminated the threat. It appeared that the rescue mission would be a success, much to his relief. His prediction came true as the gateway reopened and the humans accompanied by the former prisoners, began entering.

Suddenly, Gabriel was seized by a cloud of dark energy, one that seemed to be draining his own energy reserves. Gabriel spotted Paul and the look of intense concern on his face. He knew Paul would want to help, but the entity that engulfed Gabriel would probably kill Paul. The safety of the prisoners and completion of the mission were much more important, so Gabriel waved Paul away. He watched as Paul reluctantly entered the gateway, which quickly closed behind him. At least the humans made it back safely, which brought Gabriel some small measure of comfort.

His own predicament was much more tenuous, as he struggled to keep the black cloud from draining him of energy. His efforts proved futile, as he grew weaker and weaker, his human form turning to a wispy ghost-like figure. As his energy drained away, Gabriel sensed a corresponding increase of power in the black entity. Even if he could contact Raphael, there would be nothing the other angel could do. Raphael could even end up as he was. Gabriel's mood turned towards resignation as he was reduced to a tiny blue glowing ball of energy.

Black released the angel, Gabriel, after having drained almost all of his energy. When it had engulfed the energy source, Black had been able to sense what this being was and even its name. Once, a very long time ago, Black had allowed the angel known as Raphael to capture him and use Black's dark energy to power a primitive device known as the Ark of the Covenant. It had learned much about the primitive humans, the demons and the angels that existed there on Earth during that time. Eventually, Black had become aware of a new species called the Skarzi and left the Earth to investigate.

Whatever energy the angel Gabriel had left, was inconsequential to Black. Satiated, Black drifted up and through the ceiling, passing back up the cavern roof and onto the Martian surface. Black pondered his next move, as he drifted along the surface of Mars. There was something about the third planet Earth that might need reassessing, but something jogged Black's memory. When it had drained the demon Lilith of her energy, some three thousand years ago, one of Lilith's memories concerned a powerful being called Lucifer. Somewhere in this solar system, this being called Lucifer existed. Black could only guess as to where, but it had always sensed something special about the moon orbiting the planet Earth. Black began drifting up, into the Martian atmosphere, on its way to Earth and its orbiting moon.

Gabriel drifted around the lab, no more than just a tiny blue orb now. With virtually no energy left, Gabriel would himself be a prisoner of Mars, unable to open a gateway. It would take some time to regain enough energy to open one, given the inadequate power sources of the Skarzi. Dejected and worried about what would happen to Earth and Paul,

Gabriel drifted aimlessly. Just as he was about to give up completely, a white cloud appeared and coalesced into the image of a woman with long dark hair, wearing a long white gown that seemed to be embroidered with what looked to be real stars. Gabriel passed it off as a delusion caused by his energy drain, until the woman began speaking to him.

"Hello, Gabriel. My name is Celestra. I'm sorry that Black has caused you so much distress", said Celestra. She had watched as Black drained the energy from the now tiny orb floating before her. Celestra had known immediately who the being was as it was drained. The being was known as Gabriel, formerly Annunaki, before ascending to a higher state of being. Celestra knew instantly, everything about any creature created by her father, the Creator, just by looking at it.

"What are you?" said Gabriel weakly, barely able to speak.

"I am the daughter of the Creator, the same Creator that created you, the Annunaki and countless other races, including the Skarzi. The one that attacked you is a being from the dark matter universe. Its name would be incomprehensible to you, but it has taken the name "Black" for simplicity", replied Celestra.

"Why are you here?" asked Gabriel.

"I'm here for many reasons. The first would be to clean up after Black", replied Celestra, as she glanced around the room. Her gaze settled on the glass chamber and the neat, clean doorway that had been cut out of it. Her gaze shifted towards the two dead Skarzi guards. Here they are, still fighting after so many millennia, thought Celestra to herself. The dead guards had been killed by technology the ancient Annunaki had once used. There seemed to be some technology transfer taking place. Even the use of a gateway to arrive here would've been beyond the normal progress rate of human technology. It was most interesting. She briefly concentrated on the two guards and a golden glow began to envelop the bodies. Moments later, the guards began to stir and sat up. Unsteady, they rose to their feet, looked at the enclosure, saw the prisoners gone and immediately left the lab, presumably to sound the alarm.

Gabriel, floating in the air, watched with disbelief as the guards stood up, unharmed. They were obviously dead from being shot, but now they lived.

"Why did you resurrect the Skarzi guards?" asked an incredulous Gabriel.

"You are all the Creator's children, even the Skarzi. Fighting serves no purpose, except to delay advancement as a species. While I see the reasoning behind the human decision to kill the guards, I cannot condone it. In time, human and Skarzi will learn to coexist together, but not without much loss of life on either side. That is for another time. My interest and concern is for the present", said Celestra, as she waved her hand, sending a burst of incredible energy towards Gabriel.

The tiny blue orb that was Gabriel, seemed to shiver with fear, as the energy burst struck. At first, Gabriel thought he would be destroyed, but incredibly, the energy burst rejuvenated him, giving him back all the energy taken by Black and then some.

"How do you feel?" asked a smiling Celestra.

"I feel wonderful. Thank you, Celestra", replied a surprisingly reinvigorated Gabriel.

"You're welcome. As I said, there is clean up to be done in the wake of Black", said Celestra, as she once again looked towards the enclosure.

"I see Valinor has kept to his military roots", said a knowing Celestra.

"How do you know that name?" asked a mystified Gabriel.

"I once saved Valinor's life during a space battle between Annunaki and Skarzi. I also know his current incarnation as Paul Cross. He's a most interesting life form", replied Celestra.

Gabriel was taken aback at first with the admission from Celestra, but did seem to remember a story about Valinor being lost in battle, but then being miraculously discovered alive. Gabriel had also detected something more than just interest in Paul.

Yes, there was something deeper there, but before he could inquire further, Celestra spoke.

"I see the humans have discovered Annunaki technology. Was that with your help?" asked a curious Celestra.

"Yes. It was decided long ago to give certain humans an edge in their fight against humans who have joined with the demons", replied Gabriel.

"I see. It seems to serve the Creator's purpose whether you know it or not. Balance between good and evil must be maintained", said Celestra.

"We only give that technology to humans who will use it in a positive way", replied a defensive Gabriel.

"Commendable, but I'll have to reserve judgment for now. I must take my leave now and continue following Black. We will discuss this more later, since I will be remaining in this solar system until I feel that things are progressing as they should. Rest assured, we will meet again Gabriel", said Celestra, as she faded away leaving only Gabriel in the lab.

Gabriel, his energy and human form restored, looked around the lab. The Skarzi won't take this prisoner rescue lightly. In fact, Gabriel suspected that plans were already underway to ready the ships orbiting in the Asteroid Belt for war. The Skarzi, having successfully destroyed the above ground installations at Area 51, would clearly view themselves as superior to the humans. There was only one man capable of helping the humans and he was in cryosleep. With no time to waste, Gabriel opened a gateway to Antarctica. Stepping through, his only thought was how he was going to explain all this to Raphael.

Chapter 34: The Return

Maggie sat on a nearby lab chair, waiting anxiously for the portal to reopen and for Paul to emerge. It was getting close to reactivation time and the anticipation was gnawing away inside her. She shifted her position in the chair, finding it extremely difficult to remain waiting.

"Don't worry Maggie. I have full confidence in the team and their abilities. They'll be okay", said Martin, placing his hand on Maggie's shoulder to reassure her.

"Thank you, Martin", replied Maggie, whose thoughts were focused primarily on Paul's safe return.

Martin could see the anxiety and worry on her face and he felt for her. His words weren't meant just for Maggie, Natasha also sat nearby and he saw an equal measure of anxiety on her face as she waited for Bob's return. Martin gave her a reassuring smile.

"Hiram, how do we look?" asked Martin.

"QASM modules fully recharged and the portal will reopen in a few minutes", replied Hiram. His glasses slid down his nose, prompting him to push them back up.

"Thank you, Hiram", said Martin. These next few minutes were going to pass excruciatingly slow for everyone waiting.

Minutes later, Martin watched as the TimeBridge portal energized on cue, felt the familiar energy pulse and watched as the portal stabilized. Not long after, the team started stepping out from the open portal. Scott and his father, General Esterbrook, were the first to exit, followed by the two security guards and the rest of the rescue team, with Paul being the last to exit. The TimeBridge portal closed soon after and a collective sigh of relief could be heard.

"Welcome back, Bob. Glad to have you back, safe and sound. I have a medical team standing by to check the three of you out", said Martin, as he shook Bob's hand.

"Thank you, Martin and all your team for what you've accomplished. It was a pretty audacious plan and surprisingly, it worked. You and your team were the only ones that could've pulled off something of this magnitude. I have to be honest though, it was tough trying to remain positive", replied General Esterbrook, as he released Martin's hand.

Natasha rose from her chair and walked over to General Esterbrook. "Welcome back, General", said a relieved Natasha, as she broke protocol and gave the General a hug.

Martin felt a twinge of jealousy at seeing the hug, but it quickly passed as Natasha pulled away and returned to stand next to him.

"What's the situation at Area 51? Are there many survivors?" asked the General, a concerned tone in his voice.

"I'm afraid that most of the above ground structures have been destroyed and there's a significant amount of casualties. It could have been worse though. There was some sort of intervention by five unknown aircraft that effectively stopped the Skarzi and destroyed many of their spacecraft. It appears that it may have caused the Skarzi to retreat back to Mars", said Martin. He needed to tread carefully here and not divulge where he suspected those five aircraft came from.

"Mars?" Is that where we were being held?" asked the General.

"Yes. We were able to re-purpose the TimeBridge equipment and generate a portal to Mars. The Skarzi as they are called, apparently have an advanced underground civilization there", replied Martin.

"I see. Again, only and your team could've done it, Martin. Thank you", said the General.

After exiting the gateway, Paul had scanned the room and seeing Maggie, he immediately walked over to her. Maggie, already out of her chair, threw her arms around him and felt all her anxiety melt away. They stood there, basking in each other's embrace for a few moments, before Paul pulled away.

"What's wrong?" asked Maggie, seeing the concern etched on Paul's face.

"I'm worried about Gabriel. Just before I entered the gateway to return, I saw a black cloud engulfing him. He was clearly struggling against it, but motioned for me to go", replied Paul, clearly worried about his friend.

"Raphael might be able to help", offered Maggie.

"It's worth a shot", said Paul, hope beginning to form inside him.

"First things first, though", said Paul, as he pulled Maggie along to greet the General.

"Welcome back, General", said Paul, as he shook the General's hand.

"Thank you, Paul. Our thanks for helping rescue us", replied General Esterbrook.

"You're welcome. The Skarzi probably won't take this lightly and will most likely retaliate", replied Paul.

"Yes. That's the big concern now. Given their level of technology, there isn't much we can do to defend ourselves. If they have even more resources to draw on, then we could be facing total annihilation", said the General, his tone setting a somber mood around the lab.

"Well, I think we need to get the General and his security team checked out. We can discuss defensive options after", said Martin, trying to break the gloom that seemed to be descending upon the lab.

"Yes, Martin's right. We should get checked out first. We appear to have some sort implant inserted into our forearms", replied the General, lifting his arm up.

"Dr. Curtis will have whatever it is taken out immediately", replied Martin, concern for his friend and the security guards etched on his face. Just then, the medical team arrived to escort the General and his team to the facility hospital.

"Thanks again for everything Martin", said the General, as he was escorted away.

Martin felt relief that that the mission had been such a success. He also felt a sense of gratification, as he watched Bob and his team leave, with Scott walking alongside his father. Martin was pretty sure

Bob was right. There wasn't much anyone could do if the Skarzi decided to attack. They had seemingly kicked the proverbial hornet's nest and now would see what the result was.

"Martin, Maggie and I are going to get some rest now. Have Eva let us know if you need us", said a tired Paul.

"By all means, get some rest Paul. You and the rest of the team deserve it. Fantastic job and a huge thank you", replied Martin with a warm smile.

"Thank you, Martin", said Paul as he and Maggie left the lab.

Martin watched the two of them leave, wondering if Paul had some other surprise up his sleeve. He'd already been surprised by the five spacecraft intervening at Area 51. If it was Paul, then he'd certainly saved many lives and had prevented an even larger calamity. In Martin's eyes, Paul was a hero. His thoughts quickly switched back to the present, as he sensed Natasha standing near, her perfume intoxicating. He turned to Natasha and smiled.

"Should we grab a bite to eat and maybe a coffee?" asked Martin.

"Yes, I could use a nice cup of coffee right now", replied Natasha a rather coy look in her eyes.

"Hiram, lock down the lab for now. You did a fantastic job and we all owe you our thanks. We'll talk more tomorrow. Get some rest", said Martin, trying not to keep Natasha waiting.

"Thank you, Martin. I will", said a tired Hiram, stifling a yawn.

Martin escorted Natasha out of the lab, waving to Hiram as they left, grateful for a brief respite from what looked like a very difficult road ahead.

Chapter 35: Visit to Hell

Celestra left the angel Gabriel on Mars, confident that he could manage on his own after restoring his depleted energy reserves. During their brief encounter, Celestra had learned much about the two factions, demons and angels who had been at war with one another since their Ascension. It wasn't the first time that a race had ascended to a higher state of being, but the process of ascension had been unique to the Annunaki. They had used advanced technology to shed their mortal coil, in favor of a pure energy state that also allowed them to take human form. It was an impressive accomplishment, so Celestra decided to take a closer look at the two cultures. Their conflict, rooted in the distant past had been a result of a rebellion led by the scientist named Asmodeus. That would be her first stop, as she began phasing out of our current dimension and re-emerging in Hell, the dimension occupied by the demon faction.

Hell greeted Celestra, with its ruddy red sky, boiling lava pits and air thick with steam. She glanced around, spotting numerous life forms called demons lounging around lava pits. They appeared to be tormenting the hapless souls of humans relegated to Hell for their actions in life. While she couldn't condone such activities, the system of relegating souls to either Heaven or Hell seemed to work. She remained unfazed by the hellish conditions that surrounded her. It was all meaningless to her, considering the fact that she had created whole worlds like this in many places across the universe. It also helped that she was the daughter of the Creator and pretty much indestructible. Nothing could harm her here. It was the demon residents that should be afraid.

It's a pretty bleak world, she thought to herself, as she approached the lava pools and lounging demons. That the rebellious Annunaki had chosen to settle here was a tribute to their tenacity. Then again, they didn't have much choice after the failed rebellion, this being their prison sentence. Black, sooty soil tried valiantly to cling to her pristine white gown and discolor it, but it was a doomed attempt. Her gown repelled everything that tried to adhere to it. She strode alongside the lava pools, passing demons torturing their human captives and demons lounging around the edges. Demons spotted her, but couldn't believe their demon eyes, thinking that Asmodeus had sent them a present. The demons began circling her, drooling with anticipation, their ravenous eyes fixed on her otherworldly beauty. Soon, she found herself surrounded by fifty drooling demons, each one vying for the chance to visit all manner of torture and lust upon her.

Celestra stopped and smiled at the demons, who immediately lunged at her, some with claws extended for maximum evisceration, others seeking to grasp and carry her away. Just as the demon claws were about to rend her to a bloody pulp, a brief thought crossed her mind and the demons disappeared, transported to a faraway place.. The demons were in fact still alive but for them they found themselves in a real Hell. Surrounded by majestic waterfalls, tall mountains, majestic trees, golden sunshine and a land full of wild flowers, the demons were completely disoriented. Soon they fell to wailing and mourning the loss of their beloved Hell.

"Probably not what they expected", Celestra said to herself as her eyes locked onto the black, twin obsidian spires of the demon palace in the distance.

Celestra faded from the dark plains and lava pits of Hell, reappearing inside the black, obsidian palace. This is where the King of Demons lived, the one called Asmodeus, as she had gathered from Gabriel's thoughts. She made her way into the Great Hall, tall, black obsidian columns lining either side. She paused, seeing the Throne of Fire before her with the one known as Asmodeus sitting upon it. Demons sprang from behind the columns, talons extended, hoping to stop her. In a blink of an eye they vanished, only to find themselves transported far from the palace. They joined their brethren who had tried to attack her earlier, surrounded by the beauty of nature, tall trees, green meadows, waterfalls and majestic mountains. These demons also fell to their knees, wailing and screaming at the beauty surrounding them. For them, this was true Hell.

"Who are you? Why are you here?" questioned Asmodeus, his talons raking the arms of his throne, sending flaming sparks into the air. The woman was exceedingly beautiful, if she really was a woman. Asmodeus wasn't so sure after hearing reports of what she did at the lava pits. Now, she had even done the same here in his throne room. Suddenly, he felt something brush against his mind. It felt like a slight breeze and a memory was revealed. It was a memory of him and Lilith talking with his master

Lucifer. Why this memory would suddenly appear mystified him. Narrowing his dark, demon eyes, he stared maliciously at the woman. It was becoming obvious that he was dealing with a powerful being of some sort, so he suppressed his anger and waited for the woman's reply.

Celestra smiled at the change in the demeanor of Asmodeus. Her opening of his memories had revealed much to her and verified her suspicions. Her brother, Lucifer, had been and probably still was manipulating both Demon and Skarzi for his own purposes.

"My brother's taint is upon you", replied Celestra, as she spotted a ghost-like figure drifting among the obsidian columns. It was the one called Lilith and Celestra could see that she too was a victim of Black's appetite for energy. As she did for Gabriel, she did for Lilith, rejuvenating her energy reserves. Lilith, hiding behind an obsidian column, was hidden from the eyes of Asmodeus, who continued trying to interrogate the strange woman.

"Taint? What taint? What's this about a brother?" Asmodeus was beginning to think the woman crazy, when she shocked him.

"I know you, Asmodeus, once known as Annunaki. Rebel leader, slayer of Valinor and Shaynor. My brother, Lucifer is using you to further his plans of escape and subjugation of the humans", replied Celestra, her patience growing thin.

Asmodeus leaned back in his Throne of Fire, the woman's words giving him pause. She knew his Master, Lucifer and claimed to be his sister, which if true, made her a very powerful being. She had also seemed to know that he had once been Annunaki, the word re-opening old wounds, triggering anger and thoughts of vengeance against the angels. She also seemed to know about Valinor and Shaynor. Asmodeus decided to test this decidedly beautiful creature by sending flames of fire towards the woman. The flames never reached the woman, when halfway there, the white hot flames turned to white daisies and fell to the ground littering the black surface with a carpet of white. Asmodeus recoiled in shock at the apparent power of the woman. Indeed, she may well be as powerful as his Master, he thought to himself.

Celestra had seen enough of Hell, its inhabitants and their feeble attempts to destroy her. Her mission in Hell had been brief, but had served as a warning to Asmodeus and with a flash of blinding light, she was gone. Asmodeus sat there stunned, both sensing the power that the woman wielded and having seen it first hand. He was glad to be here in Hell, far away from his Master and this woman when they eventually met. That was one confrontation he wanted no part of.

Lilith had found herself wandering among the Throne room, just as the strange woman entered it. She cowered behind an obsidian column, after seeing what the strange woman had done to the demons. Moments later, there was a flash and something strange happened to Lilith. She felt a sudden, tremendous influx of energy and found herself suddenly restored to her former sensuous, voluptuous beauty. She had been healed by the strange woman and was no longer the wispy, ghost-like waif that Asmodeus had wielded power over.

Asmodeus sat there processing what had transpired. The woman had mentioned his Master, disappeared and Lilith had emerged from behind an obsidian column, voluptuous and somehow restored to her former self. Asmodeus wasn't happy. No one comes to Hell and does what that woman did. Fuming, Asmodeus felt violated, his anger building until Lilith stepped before him. He shunted his anger aside, as his desire for Lilith overwhelmed him. Stepping off his throne, he was about to scoop Lilith up into his scaled arms, when she put her hand up and stopped him in his tracks.

"Not now, my Love. I'm tired and need some rest", said a reawakened Lilith. From now on things are going to be different around here, she promised to herself, as she turned and went to their bed-chamber.

Asmodeus, alone in the throne room was taken aback. This was something new to him. Normally, Lilith would be fully compliant and aquiescing to all his demands. He was, after all, her creator. It had been long ago, back when he was Chief Scientist and after the Annunaki had first come to Earth. It had been before the rebellion and their eventual Ascension, in a time when the Annunaki were treated as gods by the humans. Lilith was his first creation, a hybrid merging of human and Annunaki DNA. She had worked out so well, that the other Annunaki had come to him for their hybrid versions. Then, other Annunaki decided to bypass his biological process and tried mating with humans, with unforeseen results.

Grotesque creatures were spawned by some of these pairings, but more significantly, hybrid humans were born. Asmodeus remembered that time and the growing furor over the hybrids. His thoughts drifted back to the present situation with Lilith, her perfume still lingering in the air. Maybe it was just a phase or the lingering effects of what she had been through, he thought, as his initial anger subsided. He returned to his Throne of Fire, contemplating his next act of vengeance towards Valinor.

Chapter 36: Surprise

Paul walked down the corridor holding Maggie's hand, a pensive look on his face. Maggie would squeeze his hand every once in a while to show her support and alleviate his worry. They reached Maggie's apartment and made their way inside, the door closing automatically behind them.

"I'm really worried about Gabriel", said Paul, once again expressing concern for his friend.

"There's only one thing to do. We have to see Raphael", replied Maggie.

Paul took a moment to let Maggie's words sink in, before responding.

"Yes, you're right. Eva, are you there?" asked Paul.

"I'm always here, Paul. What can I do for you?" replied Eva.

"I need a gateway to the Antarctic cavern, right now", said Paul.

"You are inside the DarkBridge facility and Martin may not approve. Are you sure?" asked Eva.

"Yes. I'm sure that the cavern is safe and I can discuss it with Martin later if necessary", replied an increasingly frustrated Paul.

Eva, her sensors detecting Paul's increased blood pressure, decided to comply. "Gateway opening, please stand back".

Paul and Maggie stood back, as the gateway began to form in the middle of Maggie's living room. The gateway stabilized, turning from light blue to dark blue, as Paul and Maggie approached it.

"Ready?" asked Paul, as he turned and smiled at Maggie.

"Ready", said Maggie, smiling back.

Paul gently grabbed her hand and the two stepped through the gateway.

Raphael was busy evaluating the assault robots and their performance at Area 51. After having been shut down and stored for so many millennia, they had performed remarkably well. He was standing in the midst of the robots, when he sensed a familiar presence in the cavern. Gabriel had returned from his attempt at helping to rescue the humans from the Skarzi. Raphael turned and watched, as Gabriel stepped out of the golden hued gateway.

"Welcome back, Gabriel. Were the humans successful in their rescue attempt?" asked Raphael.

"Yes. The humans were successful and the captive humans have been rescued. It was I, that met with some misfortune", said Gabriel, who was happy to be back in familiar surroundings.

"Tell me more", asked a curious Raphael.

Gabriel recounted the rescue mission, his encounter with Black and then the encounter with Celestra and his subsequent healing.

Raphael listened intently to Gabriel's retelling of the events on Mars, growing more excited when Gabriel began talking about Celestra.

"It sounds like you were fortunate to encounter this Celestra. Otherwise, it may have been some time before you had enough energy to return here", replied Raphael.

"I was indeed fortunate. The entity called Black had drained almost every bit of energy from me. Celestra also healed the Skarzi guards in the lab, bringing them back to life", said Gabriel.

Raphael considered the entity called Black, recalling something that occurred during the time of Solomon. Somehow, the dark matter contained within the Ark of the Covenant had escaped and disappeared. Raphael had suspected that the dark matter was a sentient being, which had been corroborated by Koros, the AI inside the Ark.

"I think Black may have been my mistake, in using dark matter to power the Ark instead of something more conventional. It escaped containment during the time of Solomon and seems to have grown in stength", said Raphael.

"It's not your fault, my friend. It was always the Annunaki way to experiment with the unknown. In most cases it's led us to momentous discoveries. Black though, is a problem. It seems to get stronger with every energy drain. I think the one called Celestra realizes the problem and is here to help. Although, she seemed to have other interests as well, including our friend Valinor, or Paul as he is called now", replied Gabriel.

"That's interesting. Why is she interested in Paul?" asked Raphael.

"She rescued Valinor from a suicide attempt by some Skarzi spacecraft and seems curious about him", replied Gabriel.

Raphael was about to say something, when both angels sensed the opening of another gateway in the cavern. Alarmed, both angels went on guard, ready to defend the cavern if necessary. Their concern faded, as Paul stepped out, followed by Maggie.

Paul stepped out of the gateway, gently tugging Maggie, so that she would be out of the way before it closed. Looking around the brightly lit cavern, Paul spotted Raphael standing near the assault robots.

He wasn't alone and Paul felt relief flood through him as he recognized who it was.

"Gabriel! You're alive!" exclaimed Paul.

"Yes, I'm alive and well", replied a smiling Gabriel.

"Hello, Paul. What brings you to this far corner of the world?" asked Raphael.

"I was concerned about Gabriel. I saw something attack him and he seemed to be in trouble. I wanted to stay and help, but Gabriel motioned for me to leave", said Paul.

"I was in trouble. It was something neither I nor any other angel has ever experienced. I had been drained of all my energy by a dark matter entity called Black. There wasn't anything you could do my friend. In fact, you would probably be dead, since there would be no regeneration of energy for you being human. I appreciate the thought of help though. You are a true friend", said Gabriel.

"So how did you get here? You look fine, possibly better than ever", asked a puzzled Paul

"It was someone called Celestra that saved me", replied Gabriel.

Paul felt as if he'd been struck by a thunderbolt causing him to stagger a bit. Celestra? The same woman he had recently dreamed about?

"What's wrong, Paul?" asked a concerned Gabriel.

"Celestra. I know that name, having recently dreamed about her rescuing Valinor from the Skarzi.

The weird thing about the dream was that she had spoken directly to me as Paul. She mentioned something about coming to see me", said Paul, worry beginning to show on his face.

"Curious. We are obviously talking about a being of incredible power", replied Raphael, as Gabriel recounted how Celestra had brought the Skarzi guards back to life.

"I saw the guards get shot and die", said Paul.

"As did I. She is very powerful, whoever she is", said Gabriel.

"She's the daughter of the Creator", replied Paul.

It was Raphael and Gabriel's turn to be thunderstruck, both looking at one another with an incredulous look.

"Are you sure?" asked an incredulous Raphael.

"Yes. She spoke to Valinor in my dream and told him who she was", replied Paul.

"That would explain a lot. The daughter of the Creator being here, is a humbling moment for us, the Annunaki that have ascended. We've always suspected the existence of beings more advanced and more powerful than us. I think the best thing would be to wait and see what she does", said Raphael.

"So far her actions have been beneficial and helpful, so I would tend to agree with Raphael", replied Gabriel.

Paul was about to lend his agreement, when he remembered Maggie was here.

"Where did Maggie go?" said Paul in concern, as he spun around trying to find her.

"She appears to be over at the two cryogenic chambers", said Raphael, noting that she had wandered off shortly after leaving the gateway.

Maggie stood before the two cryogenic chambers, having felt drawn to them after exiting the gateway. In front of her, lay the sleeping bodies of Shaynor's brother Jalon and her father Kalon. Memories of Shaynor flooded her mind and Maggie moved closer to the chamber housing the body of Kalon. She ran her hand along the casing of the cryogenic chamber, feeling the cool touch of the black metal. Would Kalon recognize her as Shaynor? How would he treat her? Maggie pondered these and other questions as she stood there. Suddenly, Maggie felt a presence behind her and turned around. It was Paul and he seemed concerned.

"I'm sorry. I seemed to have wandered off and found myself drawn here", said Maggie.

"That's okay, Maggie. I was just worried about you. Is everything okay?" asked Paul.

"Yes. I'm fine, just thinking about Kalon and Jalon", replied Maggie.

Raphael and Gabriel had come over to join Paul and Maggie, curious as to what was going on.

"It's to be expected. They are a part of Shaynor's past and most likely Maggie's future", said Raphael.

"What do you mean", asked Paul.

"The Skarzi won't take what happened lightly. That humans were able to infiltrate and rescue the captives will prove that they are a threat. Knowing the Skarzi, they will begin making invasion plans to remove that threat. There will be little that humans can do to defend against them and we, as angels, will be of little help. We cannot choose one civilization over the other. However, the two sleeping here before you, might be of help", said Raphael.

"Yes. I know. It's my decision. How long would it take to wake them?" asked a troubled Maggie.

"About two hours to wake and then a week or so, for full recovery. They've been asleep for thousands of years and it will take time for their muscles to regain their strength. The cryo chambers are equipped to handle most aspects of recovery, so all we need is your word to start", replied Raphael.

Maggie pondered her situation. It would be a difficult reunion, but the threat from the Skarzi required taking any chance to defend Earth. She harbored doubts about any relationships coming out of this decision, but it was time. They had slept far too long as it is.

"Yes. Wake them. We need their help", said Maggie, a tinge of indecision in her voice.

"Are you sure, Maggie?" asked a concerned Paul.

"Yes, I'm sure", replied Maggie.

"Okay. Gabriel and I will handle the rest. I suggest you and Paul get some rest. What happens next could be a rather emotional time", said Raphael.

"Good idea. It's been a long day", replied Paul.

"Allow me", said Gabriel, as he opened a gateway for the two.

"Thank you, Gabriel. Thank you Raphael", said Maggie, as she reached out for Paul's hand.

Paul took Maggie's hand and walked over to the shimmering, golden gateway and stopped turning to Gabriel.

"Glad you're okay, my friend", said a smiling Paul, as he turned back to the gateway and stepped through, gently pulling Maggie with him.

The gateway closed, leaving Gabriel and Raphael alone in the cavern.

"She made the right decision", said Gabriel.

"Yes. It's the only way to give humans some hope. There is a chance that Commander Kalon might have some tactical knowledge that might help. We should begin the process", replied Raphael.

"I agree. Let's wake them", said Gabriel.

The two angels stood before the two cryogenic chambers, glancing at one another, as each remembered their Anunnaki past and how the chambers operated. Satisfied with their knowledge, both an-gels began the process of waking the two sleeping Annunaki. Each knowing that any mistake could end the lives of one or both the sleepers and maybe even the human race itself.

Chapter 37:
Vermont Visitor

Celestra watched undetected from a darkened alcove as the scene in the cavern unfolded. Paul, or Valinor, as she had known him, had just exited a gateway accompanied by a woman who was called Maggie. Celestra sensed the bond between Paul and Maggie, a bond that appeared to be far older than their current ages. Curious, Celestra examined that bond, finding that it began many lifetimes ago when they were Anunnaki. She watched as Paul and Maggie were greeted by the one called Raphael and a newly invigorated Gabriel, just returned from Mars. The angels seemed to be the polar opposites of the demons and looked ready to help humanity, rather than subjugate it. Celestra's eyes drifted over to the two long cylinders containing the sleeping Annunaki.

There was another connection here, between the sleepers and the woman, Maggie. Both were from a time long ago, when Maggie was known as Shaynor. She had been reincarnated many times since then, but these were her original father and brother. Celestra's mind reached out into the near future and saw the importance of the two sleepers. They were important enough to waken, so Celestra gave a gentle nudge to Maggie's mind, bringing her over to the sleeping Annunaki. She watched as Maggie was soon joined by Paul and the two angels, with Paul expressing concern for her. Celestra watched approvingly, as Maggie gave her assent to wake the sleepers. The one called Gabriel, opened a gateway for Paul and Maggie and Celestra noted the location of its exit point. Satisfied with events at the cavern, Celestra was ready for the next stages of her journey here and her plan to straighten things out.

Celestra faded out of the cavern and emerged inside an underground facilty not far from where Paul and Maggie had exited from the cavern. She noted that the two were inside Maggie's apartment getting some rest. Casting her mind out, Celestra found the mind of Martin Weaver, creator of Dark-Bridge Technology and the facility she found herself in. She read much of what was in Martin's mind and filed it away for future reference. Martin wasn't alone however and seemed to be fast asleep with a woman named Natasha sleeping beside him. Celestra read her mind also and considered Natasha as a potential subject for her future plans. Casting her mind around once again, Celestra became aware of a familiar presence deep below the DarkBridge facility, which seemed to be contained inside a large cavern. Celestra faded out of the DarkBridge facility, reappearing inside the cavern far below the facility.

Vermont Guardian, wrapped in his old man avatar, materialized inside the idyllic paradise he had created for Valinor and Maggie. He stood before the humble farmhouse occupied by the two during their periods between reincarnations. Empty now, since Valinor and Shaynor were still alive in their incarnations as Paul and Maggie. Vermont walked over to the two stone benches that it had shared with Paul not long ago. Vermont sat down on one of the benches and regarded the empty one in front of it. Often occupied by Paul in between his incarnations, it now sat empty, as Vermont contemplated the events that had recently transpired between the humans and Skarzi. Vermont was proud of Paul, like a father to a son, as Paul came to the rescue of the humans at Area 51 and then helped free the prisoners on Mars.

As Vermont wistfully regarded the empty bench, it became aware of a presence approaching it. A woman with long dark hair, wearing a white gown embroidered with stars was walking towards it. At first, Vermont was concerned and a bit puzzled. No one should be here, thought Vermont. This place only existed inside the crystalline matrix of Vermont's mind. The figure drew closer and Vermont's concern faded into a mix of awe and humility. Recognition registered in the mind of Vermont, as the figure stood before him. It was a figure that Vermont hadn't seen since coming to this solar system so many millions of years ago. Vermont stood and then knelt down before the figure, uttering a single word, "Mistress".

Celestra glanced around the cavern and spotted a large, bluish crystalline structure that she hadn't seen in many millions of years. It was one of the Guardians created by her father to guard her imprisoned brother Lucifer, which was another reason for coming here. She ran her fingers across the smooth surface, sensing the powerful mind within. The mind seemed to be engrossed in some sort of introspection and hadn't detected her presence yet. Celestra closed her eyes and allowed her mind to flow into the crystalline structure. She found herself standing in a large, green field, under a warm, bright sun, a farmhouse standing nearby. Near the farmhouse were a couple of benches and a familiar presence sitting on one of them. Quite the mental construct had been created here, thought Celestra to herself. Curious, Celestra walked towards the presence, which was using an avatar of an old man with a white beard and wearing a flowing white robe. The figure was holding a long, wooden staff and seemed to be in quiet contemplation.

As she approached the figure, Celestra saw the figure spot her, with concern crossing its mind initially, but soon turning to recognition. Celestra was impressed with the amount of detail the Guardian had created here. Gazing at the figure, her mind accessed its memory and began downloading its contents. Celestra smiled as she saw how the Guardian had taken the name of Vermont, which corresponded to this region of the country. She also smiled in satisfaction at how Vermont had taken care of Valinor in all his incarnations. Yes, Valinor had died, but death was merely the transition to a higher level of existence. Valinor had been to this idyllic setting many times in different incarnations.

Celestra saw the most recent exchange between Paul, Valinor's current incarnation and Vermont. It had been one about choice and that Valinor would decide whether to come here or go to Heaven and be with friends. Vermont had always taken Valinor's mind here, upon his physical death instead of allowing him to go elsewhere. She also saw Vermont's attempt to access one of Paul's memories, a memory she had purposefully blocked off from access. It had been done in order to preserve her anonymity and keep entities such as her brother from knowing of her existence. It was a small matter now that she was here, so she decided to ignore it and concentrate on Vermont's accomplishments instead.

Celestra nodded in satisfaction that Vermont had followed its initial instructions to watch over Valinor and keep him safe. Millions of years ago, Celestra, after looking at all the possible futures, implanted those instructions into the mind of a newly created Vermont. This was shortly before it and the eleven other Guardians had left for Earth transporting their special prisoner, her brother Lucifer.

"Rise up Vermont. You've done an outstanding job here. Thank you, for following my instructions", said a smiling Celestra to the kneeling Vermont.

"It's been an honor, Mistress. I've learned much from the ones called Valinor and Shaynor, now Paul and Maggie", replied Vermont, as he stood up.

"I imagine you have. There is much to learn from them. You'll need to continue your work here, keeping an eye on Paul and Maggie, as well as supporting the other Guardians on the moon watching Lucifer", said Celestra, her mind already turning to a visit with her brother.

"Yes Mistress. It continues to be an honor to serve you", replied Vermont.

"Thank you, Vermont. I chose well. Now I must leave you and visit my brother", said Celestra.

"Be careful, Mistress. He's a cunning one and will do anything to escape", replied Vermont.

"I promise to be careful. Take care, Vermont", replied Celestra.

"Goodbye, Mistress', said Vermont, as Celestra began to fade away, wondering if it would ever see her again.

"You'll see me again, Vermont. I still have much work to do here", came the fading voice of Celestra.

Vermont shook his head in surprise and wonderment and sat back down on the bench. What had originally been planed as quiet contemplation, had now been up-ended with even more to contemplate.

Chapter 38: Family Spat

Celestra reappeared, floating high above the Earth, regarding two items. One was the Sun in this solar system and the other was the Moon, orbiting the planet Earth. She detected a fluctuation in the Sun's output energy, which could be a sign of something potentially affecting its nuclear furnace. It didn't look to be too serious at the moment, so she turned her attention to the Moon and the prisoner held there. "Time for a little family reunion", Celestra said to herself with a sigh, as she reappeared on the Moon's surface.

She glanced around and sensed that Black was already here, but far below the Moon's surface. Celestra began striding towards the remains of a long ago collapsed tunnel, gray particles of regolith lofted onto her pure white gown, but fell harmlessly away. She stood before the remains of a large collapsed tunnel, which appeared to lead deep underground. Her mind pondered the tunnel and as it did, its history became apparent. Excavated and collapsed millions of years ago, the long tunnel led to a large cavern housing the prisoner and its five Guardians, who kept the prisoner from escaping. Sighing again, she blinked and disappeared from the Moon's surface.

Lucifer was beside himself with worry. He had sensed a powerful being enter the solar system, following right behind Black. He didn't know who the entity was or why it was here. Not knowing was eating away at him. Black had done its usual thing, giving Lucifer a small dose of amusement, when it had drawn away Gabriel's energy. Then, not long after, Lucifer's amusement had turned to consternation as he sensed Gabriel get his energy back. How it happened, Lucifer wasn't sure, but it probably had something to do with the strange entity he had detected. He sensed Black approach the Moon and drift down towards the collapsed tunnel entrance. Lucifer didn't know what Black wanted or its motives, but maybe it could be persuaded to help him escape from this prison. Moments later, a dark, black cloud began oozing out of the cavern ceiling and drifting down to the cavern floor.

Black drifted down to the surface of the Moon, detecting multiple energy sources emanating from deep below the surface. Intrigued, Black flowed across the surface until it was directly above the energy sources. Insatiable hunger overtook Black and it began sinking into the ground towards the energy source. Black emerged from the cavern ceiling, drifted down to the cavern floor and contemplated its next move. Barely able to keep its hunger in check, Black surveyed the surroundings. There were five huge energy sources arranged in a circle around a center energy source, the likes of which Black had never sensed before. The five sources seemed to be guarding the central source as evidenced by the bands of energy wrapping around the central source. A thought soon came into Black's mind.

"Welcome, Black. I have been waiting a long time to finally meet you", said the booming voice in Black's mind.

Startled, Black drifted towards the center object, passing by one of the Guardians. As it passed the Guardian, Black could sense its power and gave in to temptation. Tendrils of dark matter engulfed the Guardian and power began surging into Black. More and more power flowed from the Guardian into Black with each passing second. The Guardian, which once glowed a bright blue, began to darken. Seconds later the Guardian was drained of energy.

It's blue, crystalline exterior turning completely black.

Lucifer couldn't believe it. He'd felt the reduction in energy holding him captive and struggled against the bands of energy holding him. He felt those bands begin to loosen and slowly give way. Hope began to form. Held captive for untold millions of years, his freedom was at hand. Hope was short-lived however as he sensed a surge of energy coming from the Guardian counterparts on Earth, making up for the loss of the cavern Guardian. The bands of energy increased back to former levels, making him a prisoner once again. Frustrated, Lucifer reached out to Black.

"My friend, can you do more to free me?" the booming voice said to Black's mind.

Black, having drained the energy from the powerful Guardian, was satiated for the time being and in no hurry to absorb more energy. Frustration grew within Lucifer and he was about to lash out at Black, when he sensed an energy surge in the cavern. A beautiful, dark-haired woman materialized in the cavern not far from Black. Lucifer was taken aback at first, but quickly became unimpressed. This was the powerful being he had feared? He silently admonished himself for his weakness earlier at fearing this being. After all, he was the second most powerful being in the universe and no lesser being could possibly harm him.

Celestra took in her surroundings, quickly spotting the drained Guardian. Black was here, as well as her far older and presumably more powerful brother. Lucifer, her brother, was being held within a reddish, crystalline oval shaped prison. Her father, the Creator, hadn't let Lucifer's power go unchallenged. In creating Celestra, her father had imbued her with the same and slightly more power than Lucifer. So, she wasn't too worried about what her brother could do or even Black for that matter.

"Hello, brother. Father sends his regards", said Celestra.

Lucifer was momentarily stunned by the greeting, but quickly recovered, sending forth his devil avatar to deal with the woman.

Celestra watched, as a towering being appeared before her. Well muscled, glowing red and with huge horns protruding from its head, the being would've caused lesser beings to cower. Not Celestra though, who merely smiled and stifled a laugh, as she awaited Lucifer's response.

"Brother? I am the sole offspring of a feeble old fool. I am unique and second only to him. I could vanquish you with a thought, even while being held prisoner", replied Lucifer, contempt dripping from his voice. Gleefully, Lucifer sensed Black moving towards the woman, tendrils of dark energy wafting towards her.

Celestra smiled, as Black, overwhelmed by the temptation of assimilating even more energy, began wrapping tendrils of dark matter energy around her.

"Yes, that's it. Drain her energy", Lucifer said to Black's mind and pressed Black on, convinced that it could take care of this weak interloper.

Tendrils of dark energy wound around Celestra, engulfing her, the tiny stars on her pure white gown began drowning in blackness. She was still smiling, which confounded and frustrated Lucifer, who was rooting for her demise.

Black, now fully engulfing the strange being, began draining the energy away. Or at least it tried too. There was something wrong! Black, instead of draining the energy from this being, was instead having its own energy drained away. Black fought against it, trying to release itself from the being, struggling mightily, but ultimately proving futile. The being was infinitely stronger than Black, drawing away vast amounts of energy, energy that Black had taken from other beings. Now on the reception end of such a drain, Black quickly became depleted, most of its energy drawn away in a matter of seconds.

Lucifer couldn't believe it. At first, he thought Black would be the victor and vanquish the woman. As he watched though, it became apparent that the woman was far more powerful than Lucifer had thought. Black was now just a wispy, black haze that hung around the woman.

"You've caused a lot of trouble in this universe. I cannot allow you to stay. It's time for you to rejoin your brethren in the dark matter universe", said Celestra.

Black heard the words in its mind, truly frightened now and knowing fear for the first time in its existence.

Celestra waved her hand and Black began to disappear, dark blackness fading to gray. Black cried out mentally in anguished fear as it was dispatched back to where it came from.

Lucifer watched Black disappear from the cavern and his own thoughts of freedom began to evaporate as well.

Celestra walked over to the depleted Guardian and ran her hand over its crystalline surface. As her hand touched the darkened surface, sparks of energy danced from her fingertips. Arcing energy flowed into the depleted surface of the Guardian, sinking deeper into the crystalline structure. At first, dark in color, a bluish tint began to emanate from deep inside the Guardian, growing in intensity, until reaching its former level of power.

"Thank you, mistress", replied the replenished Guardian.

"You're most welcome. My thanks to you and your brethren for guarding my brother all this time", said Celestra.

"Who are you? Why do you keep calling me your brother? asked an increasingly worried Lucifer through his avatar.

"My name is Celestra and like you we share the same father", replied Celestra.

"I know of no being named Celestra or even of having a sister. Besides, that feeble fool couldn't possibly create anyone as powerful as I", said Lucifer with some bluster.

"You shouldn't talk about father like that", replied a stern Celestra. She blinked her eyes and the towering red, devil avatar disappeared.

Lucifer was incensed. She had dispelled his avatar and no matter how he tried, there was no re-creating it again. It was if she had completely severed his ability to recreate it. No being could possibly do that to me! Lucifer thought to himself.

"I did and can do more", said a confident Celestra.

"What! You can read minds too?" said a faltering Lucifer, unable to comprehend what was taking place.

"You too, have caused a lot of trouble around here, brother. The demons and the Skarzi would be one example. The demons seem empowered to cause much suffering among the humans. The Skarzi in turn seem to have been emboldened to actually attack the planet Earth. Yes. You've been very busy. Father suspected as much and sent me here to check on you", replied Celestra.

"Ahh, the jailer sends his lapdog", said Lucifer, trying to sound terse.

"I'm afraid you have it wrong brother", said Celestra as the bands of bluish energy wrapped around Lucifer's prison increased in intensity.

Lucifer bellowed in frustration and pain as the energy bands tightened around him. Never had he felt so much pain and helplessness, even his five Guardians hadn't been able to summon as much energy as this Celestra could.

"I'm going to be remaining in this solar system for some time and will be keeping an eye on things. This is just a demonstration of what I can do, so I expect you to start behaving brother", said Celestra as she relaxed the energy bands wrapped around Lucifer.

"Yes, sister", came the begrudging reply from Lucifer. He had no choice but to agree, at least for now. Deep in his mind, where he didn't think she could see, he began plotting his escape. Freedom would be his and then this supposed sister would be his prisoner, the thought making him smile.

Celestra didn't believe Lucifer could be so compliant, so soon. No. She would have to keep an eye on him. With a sigh, she faded out of the cavern and reappeared on the moon's surface leaving Lucifer to assimilate all that had happened. Gray regolith once again tried valiantly to cling to her gown, but fell fell away harmlessly. Family matter taken care of, Celestra stood there contemplating what had to be done next.

Chapter 39:
Dreams

It was past midnight and Paul had woken from one of his Valinor dreams. Maggie was sleeping soundly beside him, leaving Paul slightly envious. Looking at her sleeping peacefully, he remembered when Valinor had first met her as Shaynor. They had been on the tarmac at an Innunak spaceport, Shaynor saying her goodbye's to her father Commander Kalon. After a time, Shaynor had boarded the shuttle followed Valinor, who closed the shuttle door behind them and retracted the boarding ramp. Valinor made his way past the shuttle passengers, who were in the process of taking their seats and made his way to the pilot's chair. Sitting down, restraint harnesses automatically engaged around his body and those of the now seated passengers. He activated the anti-gravity nacelles and a low hum could be heard inside the shuttle. A green status light came on signaling the anti-gravity drive was ready, so he took manual control of the shuttle, engaging the drive. The shuttle lifted silently off the ground, hovering for an instant above the tarmac and then began ascending into the sky towards a rendezvous with the orbiting colony ship.

The shuttle rose quickly into the sky, passing through the outer atmosphere and into the blackness of space. Soon, the large colony ship came into view, growing larger and larger with every passing second. Valinor guided the shuttle into the open hangar bay, executing a perfect landing as the hangar doors closed. As soon as the shuttle landed, he powered down the anti-gravity drives and extended the boarding ramp. Valinor released his restraints and those of the passengers so that they could get ready to disembark and rose from the pilot's chair. He made his way past the passengers, some standing and some still seated, until he reached the door. Once at the door, he disengaged the locks and lifted the door up, his eyes scanning the huge hangar.

His passengers began leaving the shuttle, most were scientists and some security personnel. Shaynor was the last to leave and paused at the door.

"Nice flying, Captain. Are you going on the expedition?" asked a curious Shaynor. The Captain was a very attractive man and her heart seemed to flutter for a moment.

"Yes. I'm looking forward to exploring a new world", he replied, trying to keep a firm hold on his head and heart. She really was a beautiful woman.

"I was hoping you would say that. By the way, my father seems to like you. Have the two of you ever met?" asked Shaynor, trying to prolong their discussion.

"Your father is a great man. I've met him before and had the honor of serving in some of his military campaigns", replied Valinor, remembering that she wasn't to know why he was really here. He would have to be very careful.

"My father thanks you. Well, I should start looking for my quarters. I hope to see you again Captain", said Shaynor, her blue eyes sparkling in the bright hangar lighting.

"I'm looking forward to it. Please, call me Valinor", he said with a smile. Her eyes were beginning to mesmerize him.

"Take care Valinor. Please call me Shaynor", she said, as she turned and began descending the ramp.

Valinor watched her leave. Absolutely gorgeous, but any thoughts of romance were tempered by her being the Commander's daughter.

As he watched Shaynor leave, Valinor spotted Lieutenant Belial follow Shaynor from the hangar and quickly followed after them. If the rumors were true, then Belial had set his sights on another conquest. This time it was Shaynor.

Valinor caught up with Shaynor, who was engaged is some sort of conversation with Belial. He caught Shaynor's arm purposefully, halting their conversation. Belial, upon seeing the approach of Valinor, quickly departed down an adjacent corridor.

"I think you can let go of my arm Valinor. He's gone", said a slightly indignant Shaynor. She had seen the one called Belial start following her and while she could have defended herself against Belial rather easily, she was secretly pleased that Valinor had intervened.

Valinor quickly released her arm and smiled, hiding his embarrassment.

"I saw him follow you and was worried. Belial has a bad reputation", replied Valinor somewhat defensively.

"Thank you for your concern, Valinor", said Shaynor, suddenly realizing that she was very happy to see him again.

Valinor, caught in an uncommon moment of indecision, was at a loss for words, being captivated by her beauty.

"Is there something wrong, Captain ", asked a puzzled Shaynor.

Just then the warning klaxon began to sound, saving Valinor from further embarrassment.

"It sounds like the ship is getting ready to leave orbit. We should get ready", said Valinor with a slight sense of urgency and in a more decisive tone.

He spotted a handrail nearby and took Shaynor over to it.

"Here, hold on. There will probably be some vibration and acceleration effects", said Valinor as he grabbed the handrail.

Shaynor didn't have to be told twice. She grabbed the same handrail and held on tight.

There was a slight shudder as the massive fusion engines roared to life and began accelerating the colony ship towards the jump point, some one hundred million miles away. The shudder had almost knocked Shaynor off her feet, but Valinor had grabbed her waist with his free hand and steadied her. The acceleration had begun pushing Shaynor closer to Valinor, so that they were physically pressing against one another. Shaynor didn't seem to mind it at all and realized that she liked being near him. Valinor on the other hand, felt Shaynor being pressed closer to him and found it somewhat unsettling. He felt some chemistry brewing between them and knew that he could easily fall in love with her. He was pretty sure though, that this current situation wasn't what her father had in mind.

The acceleration eased and Valinor despite his misgivings earlier, reluctantly let go of her.

"I think we're okay for now. It'll take a few hours to reach the first jump point", said Valinor, unsure of what to do next.

"Thank you Valinor. I have some things to do, but maybe you can show me around the ship sometime", said Shaynor, giving him an opportunity and hoping she would see him again.

"It would be my pleasure, Shaynor. I too have a few things to do", replied Valinor.

"Until then", said a smiling Shaynor, as she turned and walked away.

Quite a woman, thought Valinor, as he watched her retreating figure.

"Quite beautiful", said a voice from behind him.

Valinor turned and saw a familiar face.

"Gabriel. Good to see you", replied Valinor, happy to see his friend. Gabriel was the Chief Engineer of the massive colony ship.

"I take it, that was Commander Kalon's daughter", said Gabriel, amusement showing on his face.

"Yes. Her name is Shaynor. Quite a woman", remarked Valinor

"Oh? You're already on a first name basis? I know that look. Be careful, my friend. The Commander is a powerful man", Gabriel said in a more serious tone.

"The Commander and I have already spoken. He wants me to keep an eye on her and keep her safe", said Valinor with a painful wince.

"I'm slightly envious, but wouldn't want to be you. Does she know?" asked Gabriel.

"No, at least I don't think she does", said Valinor thoughtfully.

"Why don't we check out the new Kyril spacecraft on the hangar deck", offered Gabriel, attempting to get his friend's mind off Shaynor.

"That sounds like a great idea. Let's go", said Valinor, welcoming the opportunity to get his mind off things.

Paul's dream faded away, drifting into another, rather important and relevant one. The next dream had been of Valinor participating in a rescue attempt of five Annunaki prisoners. They were being held on a moon orbiting a planet in a solar system controlled by the Skarzi. Valinor had volunteered for the mission when hearing that one of the Annunaki prisoners was Jalon, the son of Commander Kalon and the one that had once rescued him. Valinor, being one of the best pilots in the fleet, was given the task of piloting the rescue shuttle.

Parked in a landing bay on Commander Kalon's own warship sat a troop shuttle. Valinor regarded the shuttle with an analytical mind, visually searching for any potential issues. Satisfied, he walked up the boarding ramp of the shuttle to await his important cargo. Moments later, a rescue team of twenty-five Annunaki warriors approached. Valinor, standing in the shuttle doorway, motioned for the team to start boarding. The assault team looked imposing, wearing full battle gear and carrying menacing weapons. They also appeared to be wearing special stealth tech that would render them virtually invisible to the Skarzi. Once the team was settled on board, Valinor climbed into the pilot's chair and fired up the shuttle engines.

"Shuttle One to Control. Mission ready to proceed", said Valinor into his comm unit.

"Shuttle One, cleared to launch", came the reply from Control.

Valinor engaged the anti-gravity drive and the shuttle rose a few feet above the surface of the hangar. He maneuvered the shuttle towards the landing bay doors, pausing as the diamene reinforced doors slid open. Once open, Valinor eased the shuttle out into space and increased speed towards the jump point. Soon, the shuttle reached the jump point and Valinor activated the gateway generator on board the shuttle. Pre-programmed with the coordinates of the prison moon, a dark blue gateway began to form in front of the shuttle. Rectangular in shape, the gateway stabilized to a shimmering light blue color. Valinor engaged stealth mode and entered the gateway.

The shuttle emerged into the Skarzi controlled solar system, its stealth technology rendering it invisible to Skarzi detection. Valinor checked his tactical display and saw that the shuttle had exited near the prison moon, but not so near as to strike some other ship. Valinor let out a deep breath, not realizing he had been holding it. Relieved that the shuttle had emerged undetected and hadn't hit anything, he guided the shuttle towards a landing point on the moon. There was a small facility that sat directly above the underground prison facility. Valinor wasn't sure how the assault team would find the prisoners, but then he remembered that most Annunaki military personnel had tiny locator beacons surgically implanted. It would be these beacons that the assault team would hone in on. Unless of course the Skarzi had removed them, thought Valinor. He landed the shuttle some distance from the facility, being careful not to generate any noticeable clouds of dust. Valinor rose from his chair and signaled to the team leader that it was their turn.

The team leader motioned for his team to rise and get ready, pulling out a small device in the process. The device was a gateway activator, which would enable the shuttle's on-board gateway. The team leader pressed a button on the device and a gateway began to form at the far end of the shuttle. Pre-programmed into the device were the coordinates of the prison section, already mapped out previously by a stealth Annunaki drone. The gateway stabilized to a shimmering light blue color and the team leader moved towards the gateway, turned and waved to Valinor who waved back. The team leader entered the gateway and one by one the rest of the team stepped through. The gateway closed, leaving Valinor to await their return. It was up to the assault team now. He busied himself with monitoring for any signs of detection of the shuttle by the Skarzi and checked all the shuttle's systems. When the assault team returned, they would have to leave immediately. There wouldn't be time for any checks.

Time passed slowly for Valinor and he wondered if he should've gone also. Although he was a pilot and had combat training, this rescue would take much more than that. "Best leave it to the professionals", he said to himself as he continued waiting. The wait continued for a while longer, but his patience was rewarded with a glimmer of blue light shining into the cockpit. Valinor stood up from his pilot's chair and saw that the light was coming from the back of the shuttle. The gateway stabilized and the first few assault troops exited the gateway carrying the five Annunaki prisoners. Valinor was relieved to see that Jalon was among them. They appeared to be in rough shape, their clothing torn in places and bruises on exposed areas. Valinor could only guess as to what other injuries they had sustained. The quicker they left, the sooner Annunaki medical teams could treat them.

Suddenly, Valinor felt a slight vibration in the shuttle and quickly turned to his pilot's console. Checking the shuttle scanners he felt another vibration and saw a Skarzi battle cruiser in orbit around the prison moon. The good news was that the shuttle hadn't been spotted yet. If it had, then it probably would've been destroyed. The Skarzi battle cruiser seemed to be engaging in some sort of orbital bombardment, but nothing that would damage the prison facility. Another vibration struck the shuttle, this time even stronger. Valinor was getting worried. Annunaki troops were still exiting the gateway and the bombardment was getting closer. Even though the shuttle was masked by stealth mode, there was probably a bright Skarzi engineer somewhere, that had detected something odd on the moon's surface. Valinor stood up from his pilot's chair and watched the last of the Annunaki troops exit the gateway.

They were carrying the bodies of three dead assault troops. The team leader was the last to exit the gateway and immediately closed it behind him, giving Valinor the signal to leave. Everyone buckled in and Valinor sat back down in his pilot's chair, buckling himself in as well. Stealth mode still enabled, Valinor eased the shuttle up from its landing spot and engaged full power to the anti-gravity drive. The shuttle was rocked by a nearby explosion, just as the anti-gravity kicked in, sending the shuttle hurtling into space. Valinor checked his console for any signs of damage and found none. The Skarzi battle cruiser had probably seen the dust plume at take-off and targeted the area. It had been a close call and a few seconds of delay could have cost them their lives.

The battle cruiser began firing their energy weapons randomly into space, probably hoping to destroy whatever had left the moon's surface. Luckily, the anti-gravity drive had taken the shuttle beyond the weapons range of the Skarzi. Not wanting to press his luck, Valinor engaged the exterior gateway system. A large blue gateway began to form and stabilized. Valinor sent the shuttle through the open gateway and exited back into Annunaki controlled space. The gateway quickly closed behind them and he allowed himself to relax, while plotting a course back to Commander Kalon's warship. The dream memory faded away and Paul drifted off to quieter dreams.

Chapter 40: A Surprise Visit

Celestra found herself still standing on the surface of the Moon reviewing her progress and contemplating her next action. Her brother had been a problem, but it wasn't unexpected. The Guardians were doing their job as intended and without interference from entities like Black, they would continue to do so. She was glad though, that Black had been taken care of. Things were bad enough in this solar system without an entity like that causing more issues. She still needed to check on the local Sun and the cause for the energy drain, but there was something else she needed to do, someone she needed to see. Celestra smiled and faded away.

Paul lay in bed digesting the recent dream and the exploits of Valinor. Even now, after all that had transpired, he still found it hard to believe those were really his memories. Possibly the only real separation between himself and Valinor was time itself. As he lay there, he became aware of something not quite right in the room. He looked off to the side and saw a faint, white glow in the corner of the room. The glow became brighter and Paul blinked a couple of times, allowing his eyes to adjust. The brightness coalesced into a woman with long black hair, dressed in a white gown with what looked like stars embroidered onto it. Exceedingly beautiful, the woman smiled at Paul, a knowing look in her eyes.

Paul knew exactly who she was, having played a big part in one of his Valinor dreams. She had saved Valinor from death by kamikaze Skarzi, which said volumes about her intentions. In fact, without her intervention, his journey to Earth and subsequent reincarnations probably wouldn't have taken place. No Shaynor and no Maggie. For that alone he was extremely thankful. The question is "why is she here?" he thought to himself.

"Hello, Celestra", said Paul, as he took a side glance at Maggie. Thankfully, she was still asleep and one less thing to worry about.

"Hello, Paul. Don't worry about Maggie. She's in a deep sleep and won't hear what we say.

"Why are you here?" asked a curious Paul.

"Many reasons, but you are definitely one of them. I wanted to see how you were doing here in this incarnation. Whether you know it or not, you and others are helping maintain the balance between good and evil. Balance is critical, as there are unseen forces at work trying to destabilize everything you see", said Celestra.

"Thank you, for saving Valinor and in turn giving me my lives here on Earth", said Paul. Seconds after saying that, he felt a gentle hand brushing across his mind, revealing his past lives and memories, some of which hadn't yet been revealed to him. As quickly as it started, the gentle hand pulled back from his mind, closing off those memories of past lives he had yet to dream of.

"Yes, you certainly have had quite a number of experiences here. Again, the common thread has been the thwarting of certain plans being laid by powerful forces operating behind the scenes", said Celestra, who laid another veil of sleep over Maggie to keep her from waking too soon.

"I'm thankful that I was able to find Maggie and in doing so, find Shaynor at the same time", replied Paul, thinking of how empty his life would feel without Maggie.

"Yes, the star-crossed lovers. You always find one another across your various incarnations. There's a sort of beauty to it, a sort of hope. To quote a well-used human saying, "everything happens for a reason". You and Maggie, Valinor and Shaynor, Solomon and Darah, all destined to meet and play your parts in the Creator's master plan", said Celestra, who even being who she was, at times felt awed by the scope and purpose of her father, the Creator. She didn't tell Paul about Vermont Guardian and its hand in bringing the two lovers together, as that would take some of the mystery and magic out of it.

"What's next for us?" asked Paul, looking at a soundly sleeping Maggie.

"All I can say is that you two will continue to face hardships and struggles, but that there will also be happier times, filled with peace and love. I'm glad we had this chat. It's good to see how well my decision to save Valinor has paid off. I must leave now, since there is another matter to take care of", replied Celestra.

"Will I see you again?" asked Paul, a tiny part of him feeling sad.

"I'll be around for a while longer. I still have much to do. Don't be surprised if you sense me or even see me. Take care, Paul and get some rest", said Celestra, as she faded away.

Paul blinked his eyes, the darkness of the room filling his vision once again. Yawning, he lay back down on the bed and succumbed to the gentle nudging of sleep.

Maggie's dreams weren't as peaceful as her slumbering face showed. She was having a recurring dream about Shaynor and one that she had mixed feelings about, some good and some bad. Shaynor was on the colony ship, walking down the shuttle ramp and heading to her quarters. She had studied the layout of the ship before leaving home so that she wouldn't get lost, but soon became aware of someone following her, so she stopped and turned. A man was following her and she remembered seeing him on the shuttle. What she also remembered was how he had looked at her. It was a look that had made her extremely uncomfortable. He approached her now with a smile that seemed genuine, but his eyes said much differently.

"Hello, I'm Lieutenant Belial, the ship security officer. You're Shaynor, Commander Kalon's daughter, aren't you?" said Belial, his voice dripping with lust and insatiable desire.

"Yes. I'm Shaynor. What is it that you want?" she asked cautiously.

"It occurred to me that you might need help finding your quarters since being new to the ship", said a devious Belial.

Shaynor was about to say something when she saw Valinor approaching.

Belial apparently saw him too and quickly made his exit.

Later, Shaynor eventually found her quarters, along the way thinking about Valinor. She could sense something between them and time would tell how serious it was. Upon entering her quarters, she was surprised to find all her luggage had been delivered and waiting inside. Busying herself around her quarters, she began putting things away, but soon grew tired. Feeling a little run down, she lay down on the bed. Intending just to relax, she fell asleep instead. The dream faded away and Maggie like Paul drifted off to a calmer sleep.

Chapter 41: The Process Begins

After Paul and Maggie left the cavern, Raphael and Gabriel found themselves with the task of reviving Commander Kalon and his son Jalon. Raphael and Gabriel looked at one another, the importance of the moment not lost on either one. Any mistake in the revival process could prove fatal to the Commander or his son.

"We'll have to split this. I'll take Jalon and you can take the Commander", suggested Raphael, memories of the Commander's legendary demeanor surfacing and influencing his decision.

Gabriel smiled at Raphael, knowing full well that his friend was pulling a fast one on him. Every Annunaki knew the Commander to be a stern, no-nonsense, battle hardened tactician, who with a single, withering stare could reduce one to a blubbering idiot.

When the Commander awoke, it wouldn't be pleasant. Even ascended angels, with all their special powers, would probably still be humbled by the Commander. He thought for a moment and it came to him. Maybe he could arrange to have Maggie here, which may help deflect some of that.

"Okay, no problem. How bad could it possibly be?" replied Gabriel, as he turned to the Commander's cryogenic chamber.

"Thank you, Gabriel", said Raphael as he went over to Jalon's chamber. He was puzzled by Gabriel's ambivalence with waking the Commander. Glancing up, he saw Gabriel smiling at him and realized his friend had been joking with him.

"Your humor sometimes escapes me", replied a smiling Raphael.

"That's what I'm here for. The humans call it "comic relief". Let's hope and pray the Commander wakes up in a good mood", said Gabriel as he turned back to the chamber.

"Amen, to that", replied Raphael, as he viewed the data screen on Jalon's cryogeneic chamber.

"The Commander's readout looks good. Starting the revival process now", said Gabriel as he tapped the display. He was confident in the reliability of the equipment even after so many millennia of operation. The Annunaki had been well known throughout the galaxy for their reliable technology.

"Jalon's readout looks good also. Starting the revival process now", echoed Raphael.

"Do we have the Commander's battle armor here? Once he learns of the Skarzi threat, he's going to demand it", asked Gabriel.

"Yes. The Commander made sure I had it before he went into cryosleep. I have Jalon's as well", replied Raphael. The Commander was well-known for wearing battle armor often, even at social functions. It was like a second skin to him.

"That's good. It's one less reason for him to give his famous withering stare", said a relieved Gabriel.

"I agree. Let's hope this goes well", replied Raphael.

"One more thing. Do you think the Commander still harbors anger towards Valinor at the loss of Shaynor? If so, then Paul might have cause to worry", said Gabriel, as it could be a new wrinkle added to the awakening process.

"I'm not sure. We know that Shaynor stepped in front of Valinor to save his life and was killed instead", replied Raphael.

"That's true. Then Valinor was shot in the back by Belial shortly after, so maybe the Commander will take that into account", replied Gabriel.

"The Commander is known for his fairness and for seeing the truth in things. I think Paul will be okay", said Raphael with some reservation.

"Good. Let's continue", replied Gabriel.

With that, the two angels got down to work pressing buttons, while carefully monitoring the revival process, ready to intervene if necessary.

Chapter 42: Kalon Dreams

Commander Kalon was dreaming, since there wasn't much else to do while in cryosleep. He was back on the Annunaki home world of Innunak, hundreds of light years away from his current location and located in the Pleiades star cluster. He was on the tarmac, standing before his daughter Shaynor. Commander Kalon regarded her with a father's sense of pride and love. A large space shuttle sat before them and they stood off to the side of the boarding ramp. She was young, in her late twenties, slender, with blonde hair and filled with a sense of adventure. He had done whatever he could, by sending her to the best schools for education. Kalon had also seen that she had the best offensive and defensive training. It had all been in preparation for a moment like this. Shaynor was joining a colonization expedition to a newly discovered habitable planet located in a solar system about 444 light years away.

The planet was one of nine, orbiting a relatively young sun. It was located in the zone where the chances for life were favorable. Probes had further verified that the planet was habitable and in fact had primitive, indigenous hominids living on it. Shaynor had been assigned to the scientific team and would be working as a geologist. An important role he thought, considering that mineral exploration would be important to the survival of the planned colony. Onboard the colony ship orbiting above them, were ten thousand colonists in cryosleep, also waiting to start a new life. The ship also had another purpose, that being part warship. It was armed with the latest in defensive capabilities and offensive weapons, including 20 advanced Kyril combat spacecraft. Prudence had dictated that the ship be prepared for any conceivable threat that might arise especially with the Skarzi threat continuing.

He'd been in deep thought, when he noticed that Shaynor was looking expectantly at him.

"Shaynor, I'm so very proud of you", said Kalon in a fatherly voice.

"Thank you, Father. I'll try my best not to let you down", replied Shaynor, her long blonde hair shifting, as a breeze passed by.

"You could never let me down. I love you too much", said Kalon, as he broke military protocols and hugged his only daughter.

"I'll miss you father. I'll try to keep in touch as best I can", she replied, returning the hug with some intensity.

"I'll miss you too", he replied as his heart grew heavy.

They quickly broke their embrace at the sound of someone clearing their throat.

"Pardon the intrusion Commander. We are almost ready to leave", said a voice from behind Kalon. Commander Kalon turned and saw a tall, young man giving him a sharp military salute.

The man was in his late twenties, with dark hair and a muscular build. Kalon returned the salute and pretended not to recognize the man.

"Very good, Captain. We were just saying our goodbyes. By the way, what is your name?" asked Kalon. He already knew Captain Valinor from both his exemplary service record and from the discussion they had about the upcoming expedition.

Valinor was one of the top ranked combat pilots in the Anunaki Space Fleet and more importantly, had assisted in the operation to rescue Kalon's son

Jalon, from a Skarzi prison moon. Kalon had selected him personally and had pulled some strings to get Valinor attached to the expedition. During their prior discussion, Kalon mentioned that he needed someone trustworthy to keep an eye on his daughter, while still performing their regular duties. Valinor had accepted, being the good soldier that he was. Kalon made it clear that Shaynor must not know. He knew his daughter and she wouldn't like having a bodyguard around. Kalon's eyes regarded the Captain, sensing something in them as he looked at Shaynor.

"My name is Valinor, sir", replied the Captain, with a conspiratorial smile. His eyes darted briefly to Shaynor, who made him catch his breath with her beauty.

"We mustn't keep the colony ship waiting Captain Valinor", said Shaynor, not wanting to be the one holding things up.

"My daughter is right Captain. Take care Shaynor and stay safe", said Kalon, as he held his daughter one last time and kissed her on the cheek.

Valinor motioned for Shaynor to follow him up the boarding ramp. At the top of the ramp Shaynor paused and turned, waving to her father and then entered the shuttle.

Valinor was the last to enter. He turned, smiled and saluted Kalon, before closing the shuttle door behind him. The shuttle's engines powered up and

Kalon watched the shuttle rise into the air, carrying his daughter towards the journey of a lifetime. It was all for the best, he tried to tell himself, Out there, she would be far from the Skarzi threat that had been going on for centuries. Eyes glistening with tears, he hoped that they would see one another again someday.

Sometime later, Commander Kalon had watched the display on his command ship in orbit above Innunak. The massive colony ship reached the jump point coordinates, fusion engines shut down and the "faster than light" nacelles deployed. Locked in place, power was diverted to the FTL nacelles and they began to hum, as tremendous amounts of power poured into them. Maximum power levels achieved, the order was given to jump. The colony ship shimmered for a brief second and in a brief flash of light, it disappeared, leaving the blackness of space behind it.

It was now on its way, across the galaxy, carrying his daughter and fellow colonists to a new world. It would still take almost 2 years and three more jump points, before the ship would reach its destination. He hoped that Valinor would keep his daughter safe and that Shaynor remembered everything she had been taught. Communication with the ship was nearly impossible as it traveled faster than light, but once back in normal space, communications would be restored. He glanced out a port window at the revolving planet of Innunak below, wondering what his dead wife Kari would have thought about their daughter leaving home.

Kalon's dreaming continued, as the thought of his dead wife Kari triggered a painful memory. Kalon had been off planet, engaged in combat operations against the Skarzi. Little did he know that the Skarzi had deviously planted guided, propulsion units on a number of asteroids some distance from the planet Innunak. Meant to be used as weapons of mass destruction, they were launched towards Innunak on trajectories that would annihilate major cities on the planet. It was a fiendishly simple plan, planned to overwhelm planetary defenses and unfortunately worked to a limited extent. Some asteroids had been destroyed, but a couple had made it through and wrought their destruction on the planet.

Cities were vaporized by the asteroid impacts and surrounding areas leveled by the blast waves. Kalon's wife, Kari, had been a school teacher. She was teaching at a nearby city school for gifted children, when one of the asteroids struck, obliterating the city and all its inhabitants. Kalon had been in orbit around a planet some ten light years away, when the news reached his command ship. Immediately fearful of a full-fledged attack against their home world, Kalon ordered all ships back to the home world of Innunak.

Sadness engulfed Kalon in his cryogenic chamber, as he remembered the return trip and the devastation that greeted him. The city that Kari had worked in, teeming with life, had been vaporized. A smoking crater, hundreds of feet deep, was all that was left of the once vibrant city. Vaporized in an instant, few bodies had been recovered, none of which was his beloved wife, Kari. Shaynor was still alive though, having been sent off to an all-girls school far out in the country away from any large cities. His only son, Jalon, had been on the same combat operations against the Skarzi with Kalon. Jalon, being captain of his own battle cruiser had escaped the destruction, but was left a grieving son.

They and thousands more grieved at their own losses and silently vowed revenge on the Skarzi scourge. Kalon, while relieved that his children were still alive, had found it difficult to get past the loss of his wife. In his children and in his home, memories of Kari haunted him. He should have been here to protect the home planet, but was elsewhere fighting a fight without end. His dreams were dragging him down into the depths of despair, when he began to feel something. A strange sensation was beginning to fill his body, gentle warmth was pushing out the cold of cryosleep and his veins were beginning to pump blood throughout his body. There was only one explanation. Kalon was waking up.

Since my last book, Solomon, a few things have changed in my life. One being that I sort of retired after almost 50 years in the electronics industry. I say sort of, because I'm still doing the same type of work in the contract manufacturing industry, while working for the same company. The difference is that I'm now President and CEO of DarkBridge Technology LLC. Yes, the same DarkBridge Technology as in my books. It was an opportunity to bring my books to life that I couldn't refuse.

I provide contract services such as product testing, product debug and Seica Flying Probe services to my former employer. It's a mutually beneficial relationship, where I provide support to a company that continues to grow and in turn I generate much needed revenue for my fledgling company. An interesting way to spend one's retirement.

Writing this book has really made me think about the writing process and how stories develop as they are written. The name "Valinor" for instance, now that I think about it, is a subconscious ode to a well-known rumor circulating in UFO circles. During the Eisenhower administration, a UFO supposedly landed outside Washington D.C. and the occupants showed up at the White House. The leader called himself "Valiant Thor" and supposedly spoke with Eisenhower.

Until this book, I really didn't give the genesis of the name "Valinor" much thought. Now however, it appears to somehow be a derivation of "Valiant Thor". The mind can truly be a magical and mysterious place.

The other thing about this book is how a character unintentionally begins to take over the story. I'm speaking of "Celestra", daughter of the Creator. At first, I thought Celestra would be a minor character, but as writing progressed, she became more and more important to the story. So much so, that the title of the book could easily have been "Celestra". Then again, if Valinor wasn't there to be saved from the Skarzi, then Celestra wouldn't be cleaning things up on Earth. Yes, the Creator does have a master plan.

Outside of writing, I enjoy gardening and how it relaxes the mind, leading to many a Zen moment. Now that DarkBridge Technology is a reality, I have an opportunity to travel down different avenues of research and exploration. Technology continues to be the driving focus. I'm fascinated by the advances being made with robots and artificial intelligence. Maybe these will one day find their way into the offices of Darkbridge Technology. Do I dare say "Eva"?

Lastly, I want to thank you, the reader. I appreciate your interest and willingness to read my books. Reading a book, is an investment of time for the reader and hopefully, I've provided some measure of escape from everyday life. The DarkBridge journey continues, with more adventures on the way.

www.ingramcontent.com/pod-product-compliance
Lightning Source LLC
Chambersburg PA
CBHW070441170726
48291CB00002B/600